THE
WILLOW
PATTERN

THE WILLOW PATTERN

A Judge Dee Detective Story by
Robert van Gulik

CHARLES SCRIBNER'S SONS
New York

PRINTED IN THE UNITED STATES OF AMERICA
ISBN 0-684-17317-4

DRAMATIS PERSONAE

Note that in Chinese the surname—here printed in capitals—precedes the personal name

Main characters

DEE Jen-djieh	President of the Metropolitan Court, temporarily Emergency governor of the Imperial Capital
MA Joong	Colonel of the Imperial Guard
CHIAO Tai	Colonel of the Imperial Guard
TAO Gan	Chief Secretary of the Court

Persons connected with 'The Case of the Willow Pattern'

YEE Kuei-ling	a wealthy aristocrat
Madame YEE	his wife
Cassia	her maid
HOO Pen	Yee's friend

Persons connected with 'The Case of the Steep Staircase'

MEI Liang	a rich merchant and philanthropist
Madame MEI	his wife
Doctor LEW	a well-known physician

Persons connected with 'The Case of the Murdered Bondmaid'

YUAN	an itinerant puppeteer
Bluewhite Coral	} his twin daughters

THE
WILLOW
PATTERN

I

'Heavens!' she panted as she let the mangled head drop onto the marble floor. 'What a dead weight the old fool is! Here, help me to push him a little closer to the foot of the stairs.'

She considered the dead body for a while, wiping her wet face with the tip of her sleeve. The transparent gauze of her nightrobe showed every curve of her bare, white body. Looking up, she resumed:

'We'll leave him lying here, I think. Just as if he fell down the stairs. Missed a step while coming down, or got a stroke or an attack of dizziness. Let them take their choice. Anything is possible, at his age.'

Suddenly she shook her head. 'No, I'll put his head right beside this newel here. Then everybody will think that, after he had tumbled down the steps, this pointed newel bashed in his skull, you see. Yes, it's rather messy. You'd better do it. Thank you, that'll do fine. The blood shows very clearly on that white marble top, they can't miss it. Now you go up to his library, fetch the candle, and let it drop at the head of the stairs. Look sharp, it's devilish dark up there.'

She raised her head and anxiously followed him with her large eyes as he climbed the steep marble staircase. It marked the center of the high, spacious hall, dimly lit by the spluttering candelabra on the wall-table by the moon-door.

It seemed a very long time to her before she saw the light of a candle through the lattice-work of the red-lacquered balustrade that ran all along the floor

9

above. He let it drop on the marble flags. There was a brief flicker, then all became dark again up there.

'Come down quickly!' she called out impatiently. Stooping over the dead man, she took off one of his slippers and threw it up to the man who was descending the staircase. 'Catch! Well done. Now lay that slipper on a step about halfway up. Yes, that's exactly the right finishing touch!'

II

Judge Dee stared somberly at the starless sky. The mass of low, threatening clouds seemed to weigh down on the black silhouettes of the curved roofs and crenelated ramparts all around. His broad shoulders sagged under his gold-embroidered robe as he leaned with both hands on the monumental balustrade of the marble terrace, lit by a single standard-lamp. No sound came up from the city below.

'The Emperor and the Court have left,' he spoke in a harsh voice. 'Now the Spirit of Death rules over the Imperial city. A city of fear.'

The tall man in battledress standing by his side listened silently, a worried expression on his handsome, regular face. The golden badge of two entwined dragons on the breast of his coat of mail indicated that he was a colonel of the guards. He took his right hand from the hilt of the broadsword that was hanging from his belt, and pushed the spiked helmet away from his sweating brow. Even here on the terrace, high up on the fourth storey of the palace, it was stifling hot.

The judge righted himself and folded his arms in his

wide sleeves. His eyes still on the dark city, he resumed:

'In the daytime the only people one sees about are the hooded scavengers, dragging along the carts of the dead. And now, at night, there are only shadows. A city of shadows, died out.' He half turned to the other and went on: 'Yet, deep down below, Chiao Tai, in the slums and cellars of the old city, something is stirring, in the brooding darkness. Can't you feel the mounting miasma of death and decay? It seems to spread over the city like a suffocating shroud.'

Chiao Tai nodded slowly. 'Yes, the silence is uncanny, sir. People went about less, of course, even during the first week. But every day the statue of the Dragon King was carried in procession through the streets to make the rain come, and there was the din of the gongs and drums of the Buddhist Temple, sounded during the prayer to the Goddess of Mercy, every morning and every night. But now they have given up all that. To think that we haven't even heard the cry of a street hawker, these last two weeks.'

Judge Dee shook his head. He walked over to the armchair beside the large marble table, littered with files and document rolls. In the rear rose the heavy red pillars of the private office he had installed here, on the top storey of the Governor's palace. It was a point of vantage from which one could overlook the entire capital. As he sat down, the golden insignia of rank attached to the quivering wings of his high cap made a faint tinkling sound. He pulled at the stiff embroidered collar of his ceremonial robe and muttered: 'One can hardly breathe in this foul, stagnant air.' Then he looked up and asked wearily: 'Has Tao Gan worked out the reports of the city wardens tonight, Chiao Tai?'

The colonel bent over the table and consulted a half-unrolled document. Frowning, he said:

'The number of deaths is still on the increase, sir. Especially men and grown-up children. The figures for women and infants are considerably lower.'

The judge raised his hands in a helpless gesture.

11

JUDGE DEE AND CHIAO TAI

'We know next to nothing about how it spreads,' he said. 'Some think it is the polluted air, others blame the water, others again say that rats have something to do with it. It is already three weeks since I was appointed Emergency Governor of the Imperial Capital. And I haven't been able to do anything, anything at all.' He tugged angrily at his greying moustache. Then he resumed: 'The warden of the central market complained this afternoon that he can't keep the food distribution going properly. I told him that he'll have to manage, somehow or other. For there is no one to replace Merchant Mei. The few notables who haven't left do not have the confidence of the people. Merchant Mei's fatal accident is nothing short of a calamity, Chiao Tai.'

'Yes, Mr Mei had the rice distribution organized very well indeed, sir. He was on his feet from morning till night, despite his advanced age. And, being enormously rich, he often purchased for the needy carloads of meat and vegetables, at blackmarket rates. Too bad that the old man should fall down the stairs, and that in his own house!'

'He must have got a seizure when about to descend,' the judge remarked, 'or perhaps a dizzy spell. He can't have missed a step, for I often noticed that his eyesight was still remarkably good. Through that unfortunate accident, we lost a good man at the time we needed him most.' He took a sip from the tea Chiao Tai had poured for him and continued: 'That fashionable doctor, Lew his name is, I think, was present. He was the family physician, it seems. Find out where he lives, Chiao Tai, and tell him I want to see him. I had a very high opinion of Merchant Mei, and I would like to ask that doctor whether I can do anything for his widow.'

'Mei's death means that one of the three oldest families of the city has become extinct,' a dry voice spoke up behind them.

A thin, lanky man with a slight stoop had come out on the terrace, noiseless in his felt shoes. He wore the brown robe with the broad, gold-embroidered rims and

13

collar of a Chief Secretary, and a high cap of black gauze. He had a long, sardonic face, adorned by a thin moustache and a wispy goatee. Pulling at the three long hairs that sprouted from a wart on his left cheek, he went on:

'Since Mei's two sons died young, and since his second marriage remained childless, the next in line is a distant cousin.'

'Have you managed to read up his file already, Tao Gan?' the judge asked, astonished. 'It became known only this morning that Mei had died last night!'

'I studied the dossier of the Mei family one month ago, sir,' the thin man replied placidly. 'I have been reading the files of all the prominent families, one every night, for the last six weeks or so.'

'I have seen those files in the archives of the Chancery,' Chiao Tai put in. 'Most of them fill several big document boxes! One of those will last you from midnight till morning, I wager!'

'They do, sometimes. But I sleep very little, anyway, and those files make soothing reading. Amusing too, sometimes.'

Judge Dee gave his thin lieutenant a curious look. This quiet man with his laconic wit had been in his service many years, but he kept discovering new traits in him. 'Now that the house of Mei has died out, only those of Yee and Hoo are left of the old aristocracy,' he said.

Tao Gan nodded. 'Between the three of them, they ruled this part of the Empire with an iron hand a hundred years ago, that was in the turbulent period of civil war and barbarian invasions that preceded the founding of our present dynasty, long before this city was chosen as the new Imperial capital.'

The judge smoothed his long beard.

'Curious set, that so-called "old world". They consider all who don't belong to their group as newcomers. Even our Emperor, I believe! I heard that among themselves they still use obsolete titles, and still speak a dialect of their own.'

'They purposely ignore the present, sir,' Tao Gan

14

said. 'They keep themselves very much to themselves, and never appear at any official function. There's a lot of inbreeding among them, and a regrettable amount of promiscuity, among masters and servants— a remnant of the old, disorderly feudal life. In the midst of this colossal, bustling metropolis they live in a small world of their own, a world apart.'

'Merchant Mei was an exception,' Judge Dee said pensively. 'He took his civic duties very seriously indeed. As to Yee and Hoo, I haven't even met them!'

Chiao Tai, who had been listening quietly, now spoke up:

'The people downtown take Mei's death as a bad omen, sir. They firmly believe that the destinies of those old local families are bound up in some mysterious way with those of the city they used to rule. There's a jingle that passes from mouth to mouth that seems to predict that all three families will perish. The man in the street sets great store by it and says it means the end of this city. Pure nonsense, of course!'

'Those street jingles are quaint things,' the judge commented. 'No one knows where or when they originate. They suddenly spring up, and spread like wildfire. How does this particular street song go, Chiao Tai?'

'Oh, it's just a silly little rhyme, sir, four or five lines:

> *One two three*
> *Mei Hoo Yee*
> *One lost his bed*
> *The other lost his eye*
> *The last his head*

'Since Mr Mei died from a crushed sull, the clerks in the Chancery maintain that the last line refers to his accident.'

'In a time like this,' Judge Dee said worriedly, 'the people will give credit to the strangest rumours. What do your guardsmen report on the general situation?'

'It could be worse, sir,' Chiao Tai answered. 'There has been no plundering of foodstores, and no large-

15

scale robbery or violence thus far. Ma Joong and I had been prepared for serious disturbances, for miscreants have ideal opportunities now: since many men are needed at the communal pyre seeing to the burning of the corpses, we have had to cut down the patrols of the nightwatch. And most of the wealthy families were in such a hurry to leave the city that they didn't take measures for having the empty premises properly guarded.'

Tao Gan pursed his lips. He said:

'Moreover, those who remained have sent most of their servants away, retaining only a skeleton staff. A thief's paradise, this city is! Yet no robbers seem to take advantage of the situation, fortunately.'

'Let's not be deceived by the present quiet, my friends!' the judge said gravely. 'Now the people are in the paralyzing grip of fear, but this fear may change into a frenzied panic at any moment. And then violence and bloodshed will break out all over this city.'

'Brother Ma and I have set up a fairly good alarm-system, sir,' Chiao Tai said quickly. 'Our guardsmen occupy strategic points in the old and new city. Small posts, but the officers are all hand-picked men. We'll be able to nip disturbances in the bud, I trust. And, since martial law allows summary justice, we——'

Judge Dee had raised his hand.

'Listen!' he exclaimed. 'Are there still street singers about?'

A thin, eerie girl's voice came drifting up out of the street down below, accompanied by the strumming of a stringed instrument. They could faintly hear the words:

> *Please do not scold me,*
> *Dear Lady Moon,*
> *For closing my window*
> *On your rays so soon.*
> *But sweetest longing*
> *Is never——*

It ended abruptly in a shrill scream of terror.

The judge gave Chiao Tai a peremptory sign. He hurriedly made for the stairs.

III

The girl clutched the guitar to her bare bosom, and screamed a second time. The black hood of the first man fell back, showing his red, bloated face, marked by large blue spots. Raising his long arms in the black, flapping sleeves he made to swoop down on her. Frantically she looked up and down the narrow, dimly lit street. Suddenly the second hooded figure grabbed the other's sleeve. A spare man clad in a costly robe of blue brocade had come round the corner. The two black shapes melted away in the shadows of the narrow side-alley.

She rushed up to the man in blue.

'They had the sickness! I saw his horrible face!'

He patted her back with his long, slim hand. There was an amused smile on his pale face, marked by a jet-black moustache and a short goatee. On his head he wore a square cap of black gauze.

'Don't be afraid, my dear,' he spoke in a pleasant, soothing voice. 'With me you are safe.'

She burst out in sobs. He took in her loose jacket of patched green brocade, hanging open in front, and her long, pleated skirt of faded black silk. Then he tucked the flat box of red pigskin he was carrying in his bosom and said:

'Calm yourself. I am a doctor, you know.'

The girl wiped her face and now for the first time gave him a good look. He seemed a nice gentleman,

17

who carried himself well despite his narrow, slightly bent shoulders.

'I am sorry, sir. I thought I would be safe here, so near to the Governor's palace. I had already had such a terrible fright, tonight. . . . I was just getting my spirits back, and singing a little song, when those two horrible scavengers . . .'

'You should be more careful,' the other said softly. 'That's a bad bruise there on your left breast.'

She quickly pulled her jacket close.

'It . . . it's nothing,' she stammered.

'We shall put some ointment on it. I'll look after you, my dear. You are very young, aren't you? About sixteen, I guess?'

She nodded. 'Thank you very much, sir. Now I'd better go and . . .'

He quickly stepped up to her and laid his hand on her shoulder. Bending close to her he said:

'You have a sweet little face, you know.' She drew back but he put his arm round her shoulders. 'No, no, you'll come with me, dearie. Trust Doctor Lew to treat you well! I live quite near, and I'll pay you in silver . . . perhaps!'

She pushed him away.

'Leave me alone! I am not a streetwalker, I am a . . .'

'Don't let us get prudish all of a sudden, my dear,' he said sharply.

She tried to shake him off. The front of her jacket came apart again. 'Let me go!' she cried out.

He took a firm hold on her collar with his left hand, and with the other squeezed her breast viciously. She uttered a piercing scream of pain.

Iron boots resounded on the cobblestones. A clipped voice shouted:

'Hey there! What's going on here?'

The doctor quickly let the girl go. After one brief glance at the huge man with the spiked helmet, she tightened her grip on the guitar, gathered her long skirt and scurried away. Through the slit skirt Chiao Tai got a glimpse of her bare thigh.

A MEETING IN A DARK STREET

'Can't a doctor go quietly about his duties?' the spare man asked angrily. 'I thought those filthy creatures from the gutter were not allowed to roam the streets, officer!'

Chiao Tai looked over his shoulder at the two palace guards that had accompanied him and gave them a sign to go back to the gate. Then he hooked his thumbs in his swordbelt and gave the doctor an appraising look.

'Name please!' he ordered curtly.

'I am Doctor Lew, I live on the east side of this quarter. I ought to report that woman bothering me, but since I am in a hurry I . . .'

'Doctor Lew you said, eh? Well, that's fine. The Lord Chief Justice wants to see you.'

'A great honour, colonel. Would early tomorrow morning . . .'

'You go up to his office right now, doctor.'

'I am on my way to see a patient, sir. He may have got the disease, and he is a very important man. He . . .'

'They are dying like rats anyway, important or not. Follow me!'

IV

Chiao Tai ascended the many marble stairs that led up to the terrace on the fourth storey. Slowly, for he had been on his feet since early in the morning. Doctor Lew followed him.

Judge Dee was sitting at the table, bent over a large map. Tao Gan was standing by his side, a sheaf of papers in his hand. While Chiao Tai saluted, the doctor knelt down on the upper step of the stairs.

'It was a street singer who screamed just now, sir,'

Chiao Tai reported. 'This man claims she was accosting him. He is the Doctor Lew you wanted to see.'

The judge bestowed a cursory look on the kneeling man.

'Where is that woman?'

'She fled, sir.'

'I see.' Leaning back in his chair he told the doctor: 'You may rise!'

Lew quickly came to his feet and stepped on to the terrace. He made a low bow in front of Judge Dee's table, his hands folded respectfully in his long brocade sleeves. The judge observed him for a while in silence, slowly caressing his sidewhiskers. Then he asked:

'What happened down there in the street just now, doctor?'

'I was on my way to see a patient, my lord, carrying my box with powders and prescriptions.' Lew took out the flat red box and showed it to the judge. 'When I came round the corner, I saw a woman being bothered by two black men, scavengers employed for the disposal of the dead. After I had chased those wretches away, the woman accosted me. She turned out to be a streetwalker. And instead of saying thank you, she bothered me, my lord! When I told her to leave me alone, she grabbed my sleeve, and wouldn't let me go. So I had to give her a push, and she began to scream. Wanted to make a scene in order to extort money, of course. Fortunately just then the colonel here arrived, and she ran away.'

Chiao Tai opened his mouth to speak, but Judge Dee shook his head. He addressed Lew affably:

'I wanted to see you, doctor, to hear more about the demise of Merchant Mei, last night. I am informed that you were present.'

Lew shook his head, sadly.

'No, my lord, I did not actually witness the unfortunate accident. A terrible loss, not only for——'

'The coroner said you were there!' Judge Dee interrupted him sharply.

'I was indeed in the Mei mansion, my lord. In the

21

west wing, to be precise. The accident happened on the other side of the compound, in the east wing.'

'Well, tell the entire story!'

'Certainly, my lord. Mr Mei had summoned me early in the evening, just after seven, in fact. He wanted me to have a look at his housemaster. The old man had been going about his duties as usual, but half an hour before he had suddenly felt unwell, and Mr Mei had ordered him to go to bed at once. In a time like this, one has of course a tendency to think . . . the worst. I examined the patient, but found it was just a bout of fever, not uncommon this time of the year. Then Mr Mei kindly invited me to have dinner with him. With the housemaster ill, and all the other servants gone up to the mountain villa, Madame Mei attended upon us in person. A most embarrassing situation, I must say, being served by the lady of the house herself. . . . Well, we rose about nine, and Mr Mei announced that he would go up to his library, on the second floor of the east wing. He said he would read a bit, then pass the night on the couch there. "You have had a heavy day," he told his wife, "you had better have a good night's sleep, in the main bedroom." Mr Mei was a very considerate man, my lord. Always.'

Lew heaved a sigh, and went on: 'When I had taken leave of Mr Mei, on my way out I looked into the housemaster's room, just inside the main gate, and found to my dismay that the fever was mounting. I administered a soothing medicine to him at once, then sat down by his bed, to wait till the drug would take effect. It was dead quiet in that large mansion, normally a veritable beehive of activity. Almost an eerie atmosphere, I thought. All of a sudden I heard a woman scream, over in the east wing. I hurried outside, and in the central courtyard I met Madame Mei, in a terrible state. She——'

'What time was that?'

'It was getting on for ten o'clock, my lord. She told me sobbing that she had just found her husband lying at the bottom of the marble staircase in the hall, dead.

22

While taking me there she told me that she had been planning to go up to his library, to see whether he needed something before she retired. Upon entering the hall, however, she saw him lying there. She screamed and ran to the main gate, hoping that the housemaster would have sufficiently recovered to——'

'We'll take that for granted. Did you examine the body?'

'Only cursorily, my lord. His head had struck the pointed top of the left newel, at the bottom of the stairs. I saw at once that the frontal bone had been crushed and that he must have died outright. He must have had a stroke when about to descend the steep staircase, for I saw an extinguished candle lying at the top of the stairs, and one of his slippers halfway down. I have to tell you frankly, my lord, that this was not entirely unexpected. Mr Mei had been complaining to me about severe headaches lately, and I had warned him to take a rest, for he was nearly seventy, after all. But he did not heed my warnings. He insisted upon supervising the food distribution personally, every day, from morning till night. And patiently listened to the laments of all those noisy people too! He was so considerate! A great philanthropist. A terrible loss, my lord!'

'Quite so. What did you do next?'

'I prepared a sedative for Madame Mei, my lord. Then I had a look at the old housemaster, and when I found him sleeping peacefully, I told Madame Mei to leave everything as it was, and went straight to the Municipal Tribunal, to call the coroner. Everybody was very busy there, and the coroner could not be found. Someone told me that he was away, inspecting the communal pyre. So I went home, and repaired to the tribunal again early this morning. The coroner was there, and I took him to the Mei mansion. Fortunately the housemaster had quite recovered, so that he could go and summon the undertakers. The coroner examined the body in my presence. He found that——'

'Yes, I have seen his report. All right, Doctor Lew, that's all. I am rather worried about Mrs Mei. She'll

23

need help in arranging the funeral service and so on. Go there now, doctor, and tell her that I shall send her a few chancery clerks, to assist her.'

'You are most kind, my lord! She'll deeply appreciate that.'

Doctor Lew made a low bow, then went down the marble stairs.

'Suave bastard!' Chiao Tai burst out angrily. 'What he told you about saving the girl from two scavengers is a damned lie, sir! It was he who was accosting her. Not she him!'

'I gathered as much,' Judge Dee said quietly. 'Not a very prepossessing person, the doctor. That's why I questioned him rather closely, as you heard just now. And although he is widely known as a learned physician, I didn't feel like consulting him on one point in our coroner's report that rather puzzled me. Can you get me that report, Tao Gan? It must be among those papers.'

Tao Gan rummaged among the documents till he found the official form filled out by the coroner. He handed it to the judge.

'Brief and to the point, as usual,' Judge Dee said with approval as he glanced through it. 'Listen!

Corpse of Mei Liang, male, profession merchant, age sixty-nine. Frontal bone crushed completely by hitting newel-top at bottom of staircase; some grey hair and blood found stuck to the sharp point of the said newel-top. Black smudges on left cheekbone, presumably soot, or black paint. Left and right flank badly bruised, more bruises on legs, back and shoulders. Provisional verdict: death by accident.'

He tossed the document on the table and said slowly:

'The bruises were of course caused when he tumbled down the stairs. It's those black smudges I am wondering about.'

'The old man had been up in his library, hadn't he?' Chiao Tai remarked. 'Did a bit of writing there, apparently, and got ink smudges on his face.'

24

'If you rub the ink-cake on a slab that is not perfectly clean,' Tao Gan added, 'the ink will spatter.'

'That could be the explanation,' Judge Dee agreed. 'By the way, have your guardsmen sealed off all the sewerholes, Chiao Tai?'

'Those uptown have been closed with iron gratings, sir. Not a rat will get through there. This afternoon our men started on those in the old city. I made an appointment with Ma Joong to go down there together tonight and see how things are getting along.'

'All right. I'll see both of you later, when you are back. I have to go over a number of administrative problems with Tao Gan, and we won't be through until midnight, I presume.'

V

Ma Joong scowled at the wine-cup he held in his large hand.

'Tavern of the Five Blessings, they call this hole!' he muttered to himself. 'Brother Chiao could've chosen a more lively spot. But lively spots are hard to come by, nowadays, that's true enough.' He took a sip of the cheap, raw liquor, winced, and set the cup down hard. He stretched himself with a prodigious yawn; he had not had more than a few hours sleep every night, during the last weeks. He was an extraordinarily strong man, however, taller even than Chiao Tai. Heavy muscles rippled under his tight-fitting coat of mail. He did not wear the golden colonel's badge on his breast, having stuffed it under his helmet, to save himself the bother of answering the salute of every soldier he met in the street.

Folding his arms, he bestowed a somber look on the long, narrow taproom, lit by only one oil-lamp of cheap earthenware, on the counter of roughly hewn boards. Cobwebs hung from the low, raftered ceiling, and the smell of rancid fat and stale liquor mingled in the close, hot air. The innkeeper, a surly hunchback, had disappeared into the back room as soon as he had served Ma Joong.

The only other customer was an elderly man who was sitting alone at the corner table. Studiously ignoring Ma Joong, he seemed engrossed in the contemplation of the gaudily dressed marionette he held in his hand. Two other puppets were lying on the table in front of him. He was shabbily dressed in a pair of patched trousers and jacket of blue cotton, which matched the faded blue of the wall-curtain behind him. His tousled grey head was covered by a greasy black skull-cap.

The small brown monkey perched on his right shoulder seemed to resent Ma Joong's stare. It lifted its brow so that the tight skin turned white and its black crest stood on end. Baring its teeth, the small animal curled its furry tail round its master's neck, and made a sharp, hissing sound. Now the man raised his head. Fixing Ma Joong with a quizzical look, he said in a deep, educated voice:

'If you want another cup, soldier, just shout. The innkeeper is in the back room, comforting his old woman. She is upset, because they took away three dead from the house opposite half an hour ago.'

'He can go on comforting her,' Ma Joong said curtly. 'One cup of this rotgut will serve me for a long time to come.'

'Quiet!' the other scolded the monkey softly. Patting its small round head, he said: 'This tavern caters for simple tastes, soldier, and for slender purses. But it's conveniently located, just in between up- and downtown.'

'Takes lots of cheek to call it after the Five Blessings,' Ma Joong remarked sourly.

'The Five Blessings,' the other repeated pensively.

26

'Money, high office, long life, good health and many children. Why not call this tavern after them, soldier? It's built against the back wall of the last big house of this quarter. Across the streets the slums begin. So this tavern is the boundary stone, so to speak, dividing the five blessings between the rich and the poor. Money, high office, long life and good health for the rich. Many children, too many, for the poor. Four to one. But the poor don't complain, not they! One is enough and to spare—for them!'

He put the puppet down, and detached its head from the rump, with a few deft movements of his long, sensitive fingers. Ma Joong got up and walked over to his table. Sitting down on the chair opposite, he remarked:

'Nice business you are in. I always like a good puppet show. Wonderful how you people can make warriors fence! What are you looking for?' The other was rummaging about in the bamboo basket of puppets by his side.

'I can't find the right head!' the puppeteer remarked peevishly. 'I want a real, true to life villain. The body I have here is fine, as you see. Big, strong fellow, with strong appetites. But I can't find the right head.'

'Hell, that's easy! All our stage villains have a face like this.' Ma Joong puffed out his cheeks, rolled his eyes ferociously, and contorted his mouth into a snarl.

The puppeteer gave him a scornful look.

'That's because they are only stage villains. In the theater, all actors and actresses are sharply divided into good and bad characters. But my puppets are more than actors, soldier. I want them to be real human beings in miniature. Therefore I don't want a stage villain. Do you get me?'

'Frankly, no. But since you are an expert, I suppose you know what you are talking about. What's your name, by the way?'

'I am called Yuan, Yuan the puppeteer. Of the old city.' He threw the puppet back into the basket and asked: 'Do you know the old city?'

'Not too well. I am going there tonight.'

'Have a good look at how people live there, soldier! In dark, damp slums, in abandoned cellars, half underground. Yet I prefer those to the fine houses of the rich. Any time!' Scratching the furry back of the monkey, he added pensively: 'The poor are always busy trying to fill their stomach, too busy to think up cruel pastimes to whet their jaded appetites. Like the richards do, in the large house behind us!' He pointed with his thumb over his shoulder.

'What would you know about that?' Ma Joong asked idly. The fellow was a bore. He wished that Chiao Tai would come soon.

'More than you'd think, soldier,' Yuan said. 'There happens to be a crack in the wall behind the curtain here. It shows you part of the inner courtyards. A gallery, as a matter of fact. You may see strange happenings there, on occasion.'

'Nonsense!' Ma Joong said testily.

The other shrugged his narrow shoulders.

'See for yourself!'

He half-turned on his stool, opened the blue wall-curtain to a narrow slit, and peered through it. Looking round at Ma Joong he said dryly:

'Watch the rich amusing themselves!'

Curious despite himself, Ma Joong got up and put his face to the slit the puppeteer held open for him. Involuntarily he drew in his breath. Through a narrow, jagged crack in the brick wall he looked into a semidark, red-tiled gallery. In the back was a kind of portico, its broad windows screened by bamboo curtains. To the left and right was a row of red-lacquered pillars. In speechless horror Ma Joong stared at the tall, thin man who stood in the center, his back towards him. He was clad in a black silk gown, and in his right hand he held a long whip. With a queer, measured movement he was flogging a stark naked woman who was lying face down, spreadeagled on a low couch. Her long black hair hung down on to the red flagstones, her back and hips were covered with blood. Suddenly the man stopped, his arm with the whip remained motionless in the air. Two large birds came floating along the pillars, with a leisurely flapping of their long, brightly colored wings.

With a curse Ma Joong turned around.

'Come along, we'll get the bastard!' he barked. Shaking off the puppeteer, who grabbed his arm, he added quickly: 'Don't worry, I am a colonel of the guards.'

'No need to hurry,' the puppeteer said placidly. 'Your man is right here.' With a deft gesture he parted the blue curtain from top to bottom. It had concealed a square box that stood against the wall on a high tripod. Along the front of the box ran a narrow slit.

'That's my little peepshow,' Yuan explained. He watched Ma Joong's disconcerted face with an amused smile.

'I'll be damned!' the tall man exploded.

The other felt with his hand behind the box. 'I have more than thirty pictures in here. All scenes from olden times. Have another look!'

When Ma Joong had pressed his face close to the slit, he saw an elegant villa built on the bank of a river, lined by willow trees. Their long, graceful branches wafted to and fro in the breeze. Then a small boat appeared. A man wearing a large round straw hat sculled it slowly along the bank. A beautiful young girl was sitting in the stern. Suddenly the door of the balcony on the villa's upper floor opened, and a man with a long white beard came outside. Then everything went dark.

'The candle inside has burned out and the performance is over. Since it was so brief, it was gratis.'

'How can you make those figures so lifelike? And how the hell do you make them move?'

'I cut them out of cardboard, but I add a peculiar kind of shading, you know, and a special kind of perspective. Inventions of my own. And I make the figures move by means of horsehairs attached to them. You need nimble fingers, but apart from that . . .'

He suddenly checked himself and looked around. The door had swung open, and a tall, slender girl came inside.

VI

Standing stiffly erect, she haughtily surveyed the tap-room with large, flashing eyes. She was rather poorly dressed: a dark-green jacket of faded brocade on top of a pleated skirt of worn black silk. The jacket was hanging open in front, displaying the upper half of her generous bosom over the tight black bodice. Her finely-chiselled oval face was very pale, setting off her full red lips, slightly parted. Her glossy black hair was combed back carelessly from her forehead, and gathered in a knot at the nape of her neck.

Ma Joong stared at her, spellbound. He thought he had never seen such a beautiful girl. And despite her poor dress, she had a nearly regal air. Observing her slender waist and rounded hips, he suddenly realized that he was doing so without mentally undressing her, as was his wont. She aroused in him a strange mixture of attraction and respect he had never experienced before. 'I must be getting really old!' he told himself, annoyed.

The small monkey was making a curious, whining sound.

'Quiet!' the puppeteer rasped. His voice had lost the rich timber of the professional showman.

Her scrutiny completed, the girl went straight to the counter with a purposeful stride, the silk skirt swishing round her long legs. She took the wine-jug and let it rattle on the wood. The hunchback appeared. After one glance at her his wizened, surly face lit up. With a pleased smile he filled a cup. She emptied it in one long gulp, then held it up to be refilled.

'The wench can drink!' Ma Joong remarked with a happy grin to his companion, without taking his eyes off her. She had apparently noticed his stare, for now she turned round and looked him up and down insolently. He would have got up to start a conversation with this enchanting creature, but there was something about her that warned him to watch his step. She creased her long, curved eyebrows, tossed her head back, then turned to the hunchback again and said something to him. He grinned and took from under the counter a platter with salted vegetables. She picked up a pair of chopsticks and began to eat with gusto.

Ma Joong watched her for a while with undisguised delight. At last he asked his neighbour: 'Do you know her?'

The puppeteer twisted the end of his ragged grey moustache. 'Not as well as I'd like to,' he replied.

Ma Joong was about to make a jocular remark about old goats when suddenly raucous voices sounded in the street outside. The door burst open, and four ruffians came in.

'Four bowls of——' the one in front began. He halted, and stared at the girl, fingering his greasy ringbeard. He was so engrossed in her that he did not notice Ma Joong and the puppeteer, at the other end of the taproom. A lopsided grin curled his cruel mouth. 'Yes, we'll have four large bowls of strong wine!' he barked at the others. 'And then this fine strapping wench! Come on, brothers!'

They crowded around the girl. The bearded man laid his hairy hand on her arm. 'You are damned lucky tonight!' he said, leering at her. 'You'll have four lovers, dearie. Four good men!'

She put her cup down on the counter. Looking at the hand on her left arm, she said quietly:

'Take that dirty paw off me.'

The four men guffawed.

'Let's first beat her up a bit,' a burly fellow shouted. 'That'll make the meat tender!'

Ma Joong jumped up. He'd show those bastards! But the puppeteer's foot shot out, neatly tripping him

31

up. Ma Joong fell on his face between two tables, crushing a chair. His helmet came off, and when he wanted to get to his feet he hit his head hard against a corner of the table. He went down again, and remained sitting on the floor one brief moment, half dazed. He heard a man yell, 'My arm . . . The bloody witch!' There followed a stream of foul curses. The door was slammed shut with a crash that made the plaster come down from the rafters. Then complete silence.

Ma Joong quickly scrambled up. He could hardly believe his eyes. The four ruffians had left, and the girl was standing at the counter, as before. She held up her cup, and the hunchback hastily refilled it from the jug. Ma Joong noticed that the end of her right sleeve showed a large red stain.

He retrieved his helmet, looked down at the puppeteer and growled:

'She's wounded! That was a damned dirty trick, my friend. If you were younger, I . . .'

'Sit down!' the other said calmly. 'It was for your own good, you know. One should never mix in a fight when one of the parties has loaded sleeves. You might get hurt, hurt badly, colonel.'

Ma Joong sat down again, dumbfounded.

'She let them off lightly,' Yuan resumed. 'Only broke the arm of the bearded fellow. They took to their heels before she really went for them.'

Ma Joong pensively felt the bump on his forehead. He knew about loaded sleeves. Women of the underworld sometimes carry an iron ball of about the size of a large egg in the tip of each sleeve. Since the law forbids ordinary citizens to carry daggers or other cutting weapons on their person, on the penalty of a flogging, those women have developed a special art of fighting with loaded sleeves. They gather the upper part of the sleeve in their hand, and thus they have in each a formidable bludgeon. Through long practice they are able to hit all the vital spots of an opponent with unerring accuracy. They break a man's arms or shoul-

32

A GIRL ASSAULTED BY FOUR RUFFIANS

ders, or, if they really mean business, kill him by crushing his temple or his neck.

'You might have told me instead of tripping me up,' he muttered angrily.

'You were in an awful hurry to rush to the rescue, colonel!' the puppeteer said dryly.

The girl had taken an iron ball from her right sleeve, and put it on the counter. Now she was trying to wash the blood-stained sleeve in the basin of dishwater. The hunchback had disappeared again.

Ma Joong got up and sauntered to the counter.

'Let me help you,' he said gruffly.

She gave him a quick look, shrugged, and held out her arm for him. While rinsing the tip of the sleeve he was going to say that taking off the jacket would make things easier. But something in her cool stare made him hold the proposal back. She was unusually tall for a young girl, her face came up to his chin. Her hair was done up in an untidy fashion, but there was a mass of it, and so glossy that it seemed to be moist. He now noticed also that she wore nothing but jacket, bodice and skirt. The whiteness of her round breasts shimmered through the worn black silk.

'Thank you,' she said when he had wrung the sleeve dry. She remained standing where she was, close by him. He felt a strong desire to fold her in his arms, but realized that this was a woman accustomed to associate freely with men, on an equal footing. Watching her take up the iron ball and put it in her sleeve, he remarked:

'You certainly made short work of those scoundrels. And with only one loaded sleeve too!' Pointing at her left sleeve, which was empty, he added: 'I thought one always carried those weights in both sleeves.'

She darted him a quick look from her flashing eyes. 'I find one quite sufficient,' she said coldly.

Ma Joong was so absorbed in her that he didn't hear the door open. Heavy footsteps sounded behind him. The girl turned around. A gruff voice addressed her:

'There was no need to flee, miss. You should've stayed, and lodged a complaint against that doctor.'

As Chiao Tai rapped his knuckles on the counter, Ma Joong stared at his friend in utter astonishment.

'Happened to hear her scream, brother,' Chiao Tai explained. 'In the street just below our boss's office. A fellow called Lew was bothering her. A doctor at that!' Seeing the hunchback, who had resumed his place behind the counter, he ordered a cup, then asked the girl: 'What about a drink for you, miss?'

'No thank you,' she said. And to the hunchback: 'Chalk mine up, will you?'

She pulled her jacket close, briefly nodded to them and went to the door with that same, quick stride.

'Where did you meet her?' It was the puppeteer. He had come up to them, and was fixing Chiao Tai with a worried look. As Chiao Tai surveyed him with raised eyebrows, Yuan asked quickly: 'What was that about Doctor Lew?'

'He's all right,' Ma Joong told his friend curtly. 'A traveling showman.'

'I met her in the street below the Governor's palace,' Chiao Tai told the puppeteer. 'She was singing a song while playing her guitar. Doctor Lew was bothering her, but she scurried away after I had arrived on the scene.'

The puppeteer muttered something. He made a stiff bow, then went hastily back to his corner. He put the legs of the peepshow over his shoulder, and the small monkey at once seated itself on its top. Yuan picked up his bamboo basket, and hurriedly went out into the street.

'That being settled,' Chiao Tai said, 'we'd better have strictly one good bowl of wine, and then be off. There's a lot of work downtown, brother. We'll have to inspect those damned sewers there.'

Ma Joong nodded absentmindedly. He watched the hunchback as he refilled his wine-bowl, then asked in a casual manner: 'Who is she?'

'Don't you know? That's Yuan's daughter, Blue-white.'

'I'll be damned! She being the old man's daughter, why did she ignore him?'

The other shrugged.

'Probably had a tiff, at home. She's quite a strong-minded girl, you know. A real hell-cat when she gets angry. She's a fine acrobat, though. Performs on the street corners downtown, together with her father. She has a twin sister, called Coral. That's a sweet child if ever there was one! Coral sings and dances, and she can play the guitar.'

'It was Coral you met, brother,' Ma Joong told Chiao Tai.

'What if it was? The drinks are on me. What do I owe you, fellow?'

'Any idea where they live?' Ma Joong asked while Chiao Tai was settling the bill.

The hunchback darted a shrewd look at him.

'Now here, then there. Where their business takes them.'

'Come along!' Chiao Tai said impatiently.

When they were outside, Chiao Tai looked up at the dark sky.

'Not a breath of wind!' he remarked, disgusted.

'Downtown it'll be hotter still,' Ma Joong said. 'Any news, up in the office?'

'Only bad news. Number of deaths is still going up. Lew the Leech was there, told the story of old Mei's accident. Mei was a splendid old fellow. Lew is a dirty son of a dog.'

A cart came around the corner, drawn by six hooded men in black cloaks. The front of the hoods which covered their faces completely was provided with two slits for the eyes. The cart was piled with formless shapes, wrapped in canvas sheets. Ma Joong and Chiao Tai quickly pulled their neck-cloths up over their mouths and noses. When the creaking cart had passed, Chiao Tai said in a worried voice:

'Our judge should've left, together with the Cabinet. It's too damned unhealthy here for a fine fellow like him!'

'You go and tell him!' Ma Joong said dryly. They walked down the deserted street in silence.

They followed the main thoroughfare along the

broad canal that crossed the city from east to west. Soon the monumental Halfmoon Bridge came into sight. Its three arches spanned the canal in a graceful curve that had given its name to the bridge. The weatherbeaten bricks had withstood the ravages of time and war for more than three centuries. In normal times the Halfmoon Bridge was congested with traffic, day and night, but now it was completely deserted.

About to ascend the bridge, Ma Joong suddenly halted in his steps. Laying his hand on his friend's arm, he declared ponderously:

'I am going to marry the wench, brother Chiao!'

'I wish you'd think up a new trick, some day,' Chiao Tai said in a tired voice.

'This time it's different,' his friend assured him.

'That statement also has a familiar ring. Do you mean that bit of skirt in the tavern, by the way? She's much too young, brother! Sixteen or seventeen, at most. You'll have to teach her everything, from scratch. Build it up, so to speak, bit by bit. You aren't a school-master, are you now? Better take a mature woman, my friend, one who knows what's what! Saves you no end of time and trouble. Hey there, what are you running away from?'

Chiao Tai stuck out his long arm and grabbed the collar of the youngster who came running down the curved bridge. He wore a blue jacket and trousers; his closely cropped head was bare.

'The marquis is dead! Murdered!' the boy gasped. 'Let me go. I must run to the tribunal, call the con-stables. . . .'

'Who's the marquis?' Ma Joong asked. 'And who the hell are you?'

'I am the doorman, sir. Of the Yee mansion. My mother found him up in the gallery. She's Madame Yee's maid, and they are all alone there now.'

'Do you mean that fortress-like mansion, over there on the other side of the canal?' Chiao Tai asked. And when the boy nodded emphatically, he asked again: 'Know who did it?'

'No sir! I can't understand how it happened, for the

37

master was all alone tonight. I must go to the tribunal and——'

'Tribunal nothing,' Chiao Tai cut him short. 'The Lord Chief Justice takes care of murders and so on, at present.' Turning to Ma Joong, he told him: 'You go and tell the boss, brother. I just came from there. He is up on the terrace with Tao Gan. I'll go with this youngster to the Yee place and have a look around.' He stared moodily at the black bulk of the mansion across the water and added: 'Yee dead, by Heaven!'

'What's eating you?' Ma Joong asked gruffly. 'You didn't know the old geezer, did you?'

'No. But you have heard that jingle, haven't you? One two three, Mei Hoo Yee, and so on? Now only Hoo is left. The leaders of the "old world" are disappearing. And fast too!'

VII

Leaning back in the armchair, Judge Dee looked closely at the tall, slim woman in front of him. She was standing quite still, her arms respectfully half-raised in her wide sleeves, her eyes modestly cast down. She wore a long mourning robe of plain white silk, fastened round her waist by a sash, the ends of which trailed down onto the floor. Her hair was done up in a high chignon, and her pale, handsome face was framed, as it were, by two long golden ear-pendants set with blue stones. The judge put her age at about thirty. He gave a sign to Tao Gan to pour the visitor a cup of tea, then he said:

'You need not have taken the trouble to come here,

madam. A message would have sufficed. I am distressed that you had to climb all those stairs.'

'I felt it my duty,' she spoke in a soft, melodious voice, 'to thank your lordship personally for the most generous offer. There are so many things that must be attended to. . . . The Honourable Yee would have sent some of his retainers to help me, and Mr Hoo also, of course. They were my husband's best frends. But in the present emergency, all their personnel being away . . .' Her voice trailed off.

'Of course, madam. I fully understand. Tao Gan, call the senior scribe, and tell him to make himself ready to accompany Madame Mei with four clerks.' Turning to her, he continued: 'My men will draw up for you the most important documents concerning your husband's demise. Did the deceased have special wishes regarding the funeral service?'

'My husband wanted Buddhist rites, my lord. Doctor Lew kindly went to the Buddhist temple and made the necessary arrangements. The Abbot consulted the calendar and said that tomorrow night at seven o'clock would be an auspicious hour to commence the service.'

'I shall give myself the honour of attending, madam. I greatly admired your husband. He was the only one of the so-called "old set" here who always took an active part in city life. Most charitable organizations were founded by him, and he had liberally endowed them. It is you who are hit most cruelly by his loss, madam. Yet the thought that the entire city mourns with you shall, I hope, alleviate to a certain extent your deep sorrow. Allow me to offer you a cup of tea.'

She made a bow, and took the teacup with both hands. The judge noticed that she wore on her forefinger a golden ring set with a beautiful, big blue stone that matched the ones of her ear-pendants. He felt great compassion for this quiet, dignified lady.

'You should have left the city, madam. Most ladies did when this terrible visitation struck us, and I thought that a very wise precaution.' So speaking, he pushed the white porcelain plate of cakes towards her.

She was going to take one, but suddenly checked

herself. With wide eyes she stared at the cakes. It lasted only a fraction of a second, then she had herself under control again. She shook her head and replied softly:

'I could not well have left my husband alone, my lord. I knew how deeply concerned he was over the suffering of the people, and I was afraid that if I weren't there he would over-exert himself, and fall ill. But he would not listen to me, and now . . .'

She covered her face with her sleeve. Judge Dee gave her some time to regain her composure, then he asked:

'Shall I send a messenger to the members of your family up in the mountain villa, madam?'

'That is very thoughtful of you, sir. A cousin of my husband is staying there, and he must take charge as soon as possible. Unfortunately my husband's two sons by his first wife died young, so there is no direct heir. . . .'

Tao Gan came back with an elderly gentleman dressed sedately in black.

'The four clerks have gone down to the main gate, sir,' Tao Gan announced. 'They will order a military sedan chair for Mrs Mei.'

The judge rose. 'I apologize for being unable to provide a closed palankeen for you, madam. But as you know all civilian chair-bearers have been enlisted for scavenger service.'

She made a low bow and went to the stairs, followed by the scribe.

'Handsome lady,' Tao Gan remarked.

Judge Dee had not heard him. He had taken up the plate with cakes and examined them one by one.

'What's wrong with those cakes, sir?' Tao Gan asked, astonished.

'That's what I am wondering about,' the judge replied with a vexed frown. 'I offered them to Mrs Mei just now, and the sight of those cakes badly frightened her. Yet it's the ordinary kind of rice-cake always served with tea.'

JUDGE DEE RECEIVES MRS MEI

Tao Gan regarded the plate. Then he pointed at the blue landscape decorating its center.

'Could it have been the design of the plate, sir? It is quite a common motif, though, popular with potters all over the country. The so-called Willow Pattern.'

The judge tilted the porcelain plate so that the small round cakes fell on to the table. He examined the design. It showed an elegant country villa with many pointed roofs and outhouses, built on the waterside. The bank was lined with willow trees. On the left a narrow, curved bridge led to a water-pavilion. Three tiny figures were crossing the bridge, two close together, the third somewhat behind them, waving a stick. In the air flew two birds with long plumage.

'What's the story of this motif again?' he asked.

'There are at least a dozen versions, sir. The most popular one, related by the story-tellers in the market, is that, many centuries ago, the villa with the willows belonged to a wealthy official. He had only one daughter, whom he had promised in marriage to an elderly colleague of his, also a very rich man. The daughter, however, had fallen in love with her father's secretary, a poor young student. The father discovered their secret love-affair. They wanted to flee, but he pursued them across the bridge. Some versions say that the young lovers then drowned themselves in despair, and that their souls were changed into a pair of swallows or mandarin ducks. Others say that they had a small boat lying moored under the pavilion, and succeeded in escaping. They settled down in a distant part of the country, and lived happily ever after.'

Judge Dee shrugged his shoulders. 'A nice romantic tale. I can't see anything in it that would frighten a distinguished lady. However, she is very upset about her husband's accident, of course. What is your hurry, Ma Joong?'

Ma Joong, who had been coming up the marble stairs three at a time, quickly stepped on to the terrace.

'Mr Yee has been murdered, sir!' he announced. 'In his own house. Chiao Tai is there now.'

'Yee? Do you mean the so-called Marquis Yee?'

'Indeed sir. Brother Chiao and I met his doorman on our way downtown.'

'I shall change and go there at once, with Tao Gan. You wait here for Chiao Tai, Ma Joong. Then you two see about those sewers, that is urgent too. Get me a thin cotton robe, Tao Gan.'

VIII

The four soldiers put Judge Dee's sedan chair down in front of the towering gatehouse, and the judge and Tao Gan descended into the dead quiet street. At the head of a flight of broad stone steps they saw an enormous iron-studded double gate. In the right panel was a narrow door, barely broad enough to let through one man.

'When passing by here,' Judge Dee told Tao Gan, 'I often wondered why this mansion, located in the center of the town, is built like a fortress.'

'In the olden days, sir, about a century ago, this place marked the entrance to the city. The Marquis Yee, then the self-styled ruler of this part of the country, exacted toll from every vessel passing underneath the Halfmoon Bridge. The canal was then the outer moat of the city.'

The small door in the iron gate opened and Chiao Tai appeared, the young doorman behind him.

'It was murder all right, sir,' Chiao Tai reported. 'Yee was struck down in the gallery that runs all along the back of the house, overlooking the canal. This boy's mother found him, she is the old lady's maid. I searched the whole place, but there wasn't a trace of the murderer. He must have come in and slipped out again, all by this same door. For there's no other exit.' Pointing at the high, crenelated wall that loomed above them, he went on: 'This wall surrounds the property on three sides. The fourth is protected by the canal.'

He led them on to a spacious paved courtyard. It was lit by a single lantern suspended over the gate of the doorman's lodge, on the right.

'The small door in the gate,' Chiao Tai resumed, 'is closed by a latch. From the outside it can only be opened by using a special key, but on the inside you can lift the latch with your finger. And when you pull the door shut behind you, the latch falls into place and the door is locked.'

'Which means that the murderer had to be admitted by someone inside,' Judge Dee remarked, 'but that he could leave all by himself.' He asked the youngster: 'What visitors did you admit tonight?'

'None, sir! But I was in the kitchen most of the time. The master might have let somebody inside himself.'

'How many keys are there to the door in the gate?'

'Only one, sir. And that I always keep with me.'

'I see.' In the dim light the judge could not see the young doorman's face clearly, but he seemed ill at ease. He decided to question him closely later. 'Lead us to the scene of the crime!' he told Chiao Tai.

His lieutenant hesitated a moment or two before he said:

'I think, sir, that it might be better if you first saw Mrs Yee. Her maid told me that the old lady is very upset, and eager to talk to you.'

'All right. The doorman shall take us to her. You may go back to the office now, Chiao Tai. Ma Joong is waiting for you there.'

The doorman fetched a lampion from the gatehouse and took the judge and Tao Gan into a large, dark hall. The light threw erratic flashes on the rows of halberds and spears that stood in red-lacquered racks against the walls on left and right. At the end stood a large portable signboard with the inscription 'Clear the way!' in big black letters.

'Those symbols of authority ought to be removed,'

Judge Dee remarked peevishly to Tao Gan. 'It is more than a century since the Yee family had executive power—and usurped power at that!'

'They are just relics of the past, sir.'

'That's what they ought to be, at least!' the judge muttered.

They went through a number of winding corridors, their footsteps echoing hollowly under the high, vaulted roof.

'Ordinarily there are nearly eighty servants here, sir,' the young doorman said dejectedly. 'When the sickness came, many wanted to leave, but the master would not allow it. But after ten servants had died, the master became afraid and sent them all to the mountains, all of them. Except my mother and me, that is.'

They crossed a small walled-in garden, planted with flowering shrubs; their sweet scent mingled with the dank smell of the hot, still air. The boy raised his lampion and knocked softly on the intricately carved panel of the gold-lacquered door.

A tall, bony woman of about fifty opened it. She was dressed in a long, dark-brown gown. Her untidy grey hair was done up with a blue band. While she was making a stiff bow the judge asked her:

'When did you discover the murder?'

'About one hour ago,' she replied in a harsh, grating voice. 'When I went up to the gallery with the tea-basket.'

'Did you touch anything there?'

She gave the judge a steady look from deep-set, glittering eyes.

'Only his wrist. He was dead, but his body was still warm. This way, please.'

Judge Dee and Tao Gan followed her into a narrow passage. Her son stayed behind, at the garden door.

The maid ushered them into a dome-like hall, dimly lit by a tall candelabrum of wrought silver in the back, and by the glowing coals in a large copper brazier in the corner; on the coals stood an iron tripod carrying a steaming medicine jar. The hot, moist air, saturated with the pungent smell of drugs, was nearly suffocating.

45

The judge stared, astonished, at the raised platform of carved ebony in the rear, near to the silver candelabrum. On the platform stood a colossal throne-seat of gilded wood. Among the red-silk cushions a thin woman was sitting, stiffly erect, motionless but for her emaciated white hands, which were playing with the amber rosary in her lap. She wore a sumptuous robe of yellow brocade, embroidered with green and crimson phoenix birds. Her grey hair was done up in a high, elaborate chignon, bristling with long golden hairpins ending in jeweled knobs. On the wall above the throne hung a painted silk scroll nearly six feet high, representing a pair of phoenixes in full colors. The platform was flanked by two fans mounted on high, red-lacquered stakes.

Judge Dee cast a meaningful look at Tao Gan. The phoenix was the sacred symbol of the Empress, just as the five-clawed dragon symbolized the Emperor. And the two standing fans were the privilege of persons of the Imperial blood. Tao Gan pursed his lips.

The maid went hurriedly across the marble floor and whispered something to the still figure on the throne.

'Come nearer,' a cracked, toneless voice spoke.

The judge went to the platform. He now noticed that Mrs Yee's eyes had a strange, remote look. She could not be much older than fifty, he thought, but sickness and sorrow had ravaged her once handsome face. He now also saw that the colors of her robe had faded and that here and there large tears had been clumsily patched. The scroll painting was disfigured by ugly stains, covered with mold, and the cracked lacquer of the throne was peeling off.

'It is only meet that the Lord Chief Justice comes to inquire in person into the dastardly murder of the marquis,' the toneless voice announced.

'I am only doing my duty, madam,' Judge Dee said quietly. 'I offer you my sincere condolences. Since I want to begin the search for the murderer at once, I beg leave to forego the customary amenities.' As she inclined her head, he asked: 'Have you any idea who could have murdered your husband?'

'Of course,' the old lady replied curtly. 'It is the Marquis of Yeh, our arch enemy. He has been planning to bring about the downfall of the house of Yee for many a year.'

Noticing Judge Dee's bewildered look, Tao Gan quickly stepped up close to him and whispered:

'During the interregnum one hundred years ago, the Marquisate of Yeh was located on the other side of the river. The family became extinct about sixty years ago.'

The judge gave the maid a questioning look. She shrugged her shoulders and went to the brazier in the corner. Squatting down, she began to stir the medicine with two copper chopsticks.

'Did Marquis Yeh come here tonight?' Judge Dee asked.

'The transactions in the men's council hall are not my concern,' the old lady said stonily. 'Ask Marshall Hoo.'

A corner of her mouth began to twitch. The amber rosary fell from her lap onto the floor with a rattling noise. She rose slowly, and descended from the platform with a strange, automaton-like movement, ascertaining the edge of each step with the tip of her small, embroidered silk shoe.

In front of the judge she sank on her knees. Raising her arms in the long sleeves she pleaded in a voice that suddenly sounded rich and full:

'Avenge my husband, sir! He was a great and good man. Please!'

Tears came trickling down her hollow cheeks. The maid quickly went to her and helped her mistress rise. She let her drink from a small porcelain bowl. The old lady passed her thin white hand over her face. Then she spoke, her voice toneless again:

'I have ordered Marshall Hoo and his knights to assist you. You may retire.'

The judge cast a pitying glance at her ravaged face. Just as he turned to the door, he saw the maid making frantic signs at him behind the old lady's back. Then she pointed at Tao Gan. Evidently she wanted his lieu-

A LADY KNEELS BEFORE THE JUDGE

tenant to stay behind. Judge Dee nodded his assent and left.

'Take me to the gallery!' he told the doorman.

Following the youngster through cavernous halls and long, silent corridors with raftered ceilings blackened by age, he felt increasingly ill at ease. The meeting with this pitiful old lady, sick of body and mind, leading a shadow existence amidst the relics of a phantom-past had shocked him deeply. Even more disturbing, however, was the uncanny, threatening atmosphere of this old, deserted mansion. One fleeting moment he had a vision of himself as an unreal visitor to a very real world that existed one hundred years ago, a sinister age of brutal violence and revolting bloodshed. Was the past usurping the present? Were the dead of the past rising to join the errant souls of the victims of the plague, was this ghostly horde going to take over the silent, empty Imperial capital? And was this then the reason for the strange feeling of fear and foreboding that had got hold of him earlier in the night, when from his high terrace he was looking out over the dead city?

With an effort he pulled himself together. He wiped the cold sweat from his face and followed the youngster who was descending a narrow flight of stairs. He pushed a double door open and stepped aside to let the judge pass into a dim gallery.

'You may go back to Lady Yee's quarters,' he told the boy. He closed the door and stared at the man clad in a grey houserobe who was lying sprawled in the armchair beside the table, right in the center. The light of the spluttering candle on the table threw weird flashes on the horribly mutilated face. Standing still, his back against the door, the judge surveyed the unusual interior. The gallery, paved with red flagstones, stretched out to the right and left of the door, one long, narrow rectangle, about sixty feet long. The outer wall, facing the judge, was pierced at regular intervals by narrow vertical slits, like those used by archers to shoot their arrows through at the enemy outside. All along the front of this wall was a row of pillars, lacquered red. In the middle, behind the table where the dead man was lying, four bay windows formed a kind of portico. The windows, broad and low, were covered by bamboo roll curtains. The wall on Judge Dee's side had a wainscoting of dark wood. Further along, opposite the table, was a narrow platform, raised about one foot above the floor. The judge thought it might have been used for an orchestra, although that seemed singularly out of place in an archers' gallery. Beside the platform stood a low couch, covered by a thick reed mat, but without stiles or canopy, and evidently used for sitting rather than for sleeping. Except for half a dozen highbacked chairs placed among the pillars, there was no furniture. He reflected that in the olden days this gallery must have been a strong strategic point. From here one could cover the traffic on the canal and the bridge. The bay windows and the portico had evidently been added later, in order to transform the gallery into a kind of lounge.

Judge Dee went up to the table. A close look at the dead man made him wince involuntarily. He had seen death in many forms, but the sight made him feel sick. The left half of the face had been crushed by a terrible blow that had dislocated the left eye. It was now hanging down on the cheek by a few threads of red tissue. The other eye was petrified in an expression of stark terror. The mouth was opened wide, as if he was about to utter a scream. The left shoulder of the house-robe was a mass of clotted blood. The judge shooed a few bluebottles away. Their indignant buzzing was the only sound disturbing the profound silence.

The dead man's arms hung down limply in the long sleeves, his legs were spread wide apart. He must have been standing by the table when he was struck down, the force of the blow smacking him backwards into the solid ebony chair. The judge passed his hands over the arms and legs. The body was not yet stiff. Having rolled the sleeves up he noticed that the arms showed no bruises or other signs of violence. He righted himself. The coroner would do the rest.

On the floor, beside the dead man's black cap, lay a

whip with a short butt and long, thin thongs. Among the thongs he saw some wilting flowers, and a number of shards; they must belong to the vase or bowl the flowers had been put in, made of white porcelain with a design in blue. On the table, beside the candle, stood a large ginger jar of green earthenware, and a platter, filled with ginger sweetmeats. The thick syrup was black with greedy flies. Beside the padded tea-basket stood two porcelain cups; in one some tea was left, the other was perfectly clean. Another armchair was drawn up close to the opposite side of the table, it had evidently not been used.

With a sigh the judge righted himself. Slowly caressing his long beard, he looked down at the still figure. It was a great pity that he had never met him. For now he would have to rely on second-hand information in order to form a general idea of the dead man's personality. And even that second-hand information would be hard to come by. Unlike Mei, Yee had always kept to the 'old world', he had had no close friends except Mei and Hoo. Hoo the judge had never met either. He racked his brain, but he could not remember Mei ever having passed any remarks on either Yee or Hoo.

'Wish I could get at least an idea of his expression,' he muttered disconsolately. With half of the face gone, however, that was a difficult task. A long, rather sallow face, with a thin mouth, a grey moustache and a frayed goatee. That was all. He had been of slightly more than average height, and rather thin.

The judge heaved a long sigh. The outward appearance didn't matter so much, after all. Most important was the dead man's character. That was always the best clue to the murderer. Staring at the mutilated face, he idly wondered whether Yee too had been living mainly in the past.

IX

Judge Dee was roused from his musings by the entrance of Tao Gan and the maid. Tao Gan motioned her to wait by the door, then he came up to the judge and said in a low voice:

'The maid hated Yee, sir. She has quite a story to tell about him.' After a quick glance at the corpse, he asked keenly: 'Have you any idea yet how it happened, sir?'

'The murderer was either a close friend or a person of low social status,' the judge said slowly. 'That much I deduce from the fact that Yee, although he personally admitted his murderer, did not offer him a chair or a cup of tea. After Yee had brought him up to the gallery here, he himself sat down, drank a cup of tea and had some candied ginger—if he hadn't done so already before, that is, while waiting for his visitor. Then there developed a violent quarrel, perhaps even a hand to hand fight; you see that whip on the floor, and the broken flower vase. Yee screamed, and the murderer killed him with one blow from a heavy blunt instrument. Judging by the shape and nature of the wound, I think it was a thick club with a rounded head. There was a ferocious force behind that blow, Tao Gan. The murderer must have been a man of great bodily strength. That is all I can say thus far. Presently we shall search for clues.' He beckoned the maid, went to the couch and sat down on the edge.

The maid came up to them without a glance at the dead man, and stood herself before the judge, with folded arms. Seeing her surly face, Judge Dee asked affably:

'What is your name?'

'Cassia, sir,' she replied curtly.

'How long have you been working here, Cassia?'

'As long as I can remember. I was born and bred in this house.'

'I see. Is your mistress's mind permanently deranged?'

'No sir. It's only when she gets upset that she begins to mix up past and present.' Having thrown a disdainful look at the corpse in the chair, she resumed in her grating voice: 'It was all his fault. He was a mean, cruel devil who fully deserved to come to a sticky end. A pity he was killed outright. He should've suffered, as he made others suffer, and especially his poor wife.'

'His wife described him as a great and good man,' the judge said coldly. 'It was her love for him that cleared her mind for one brief moment when, kneeling before me, she begged me to bring his murderer to justice.'

She shrugged her broad, bony shoulders.

'I tell you that the master was a dissolute lecher. Used to have the lowest sluts from the gutter up here, nearly every day. And what for? To watch them doing their dirty dances—if you care to call those filthy pranks dances—on that platform there.' Seeing that the judge was about to make an angry remark, she added quickly: 'The master got all kinds of nasty diseases from those women, which was just what he deserved. But he passed them on to his poor wife, and that's what ruined her health. But he didn't care. Not he!'

'Your master's body is hardly cold yet, woman!' Judge Dee burst out angrily. 'Do you realize that his spirit may still be present here, and hear all those terrible things you are saying?'

'I am not afraid of ghosts. This old, evil house is full of them. You can hear them wail, on stormy nights. The ghosts of the men and women maimed or tortured in this same gallery, or starved to death in the dungeons.'

'You are referring to things that happened one hundred years ago,' the judge said with disdain.

'His father and his grandfather were as bad as him. Savage beasts, that's what they were, all of them. But I needn't go back to the past to prove that. Oh no! Six years ago the master whipped a bondmaid to death, here, on that same couch you are sitting on, sir.'

'Have you found a record of that case?' Judge Dee asked Tao Gan sharply.

'No sir. The only charge ever brought against Yee was that of usury. And he was acquitted.'

'You are telling a pack of lies, woman!' the judge barked.

'It's the truth, sir. Have your men dig up the cluster of bamboos on the south side of the back yard and you'll find her bones. But who in this house would have wanted to accuse the master? Our parents served his father, our grandparents his grandfather. He was a bad man, but he was our master. Heaven willed it so.'

Judge Dee gave her a thoughtful look. After a brief pause he asked, pointing at the whip on the floor:

'Have you seen that thing before?'

She sniffed.

'Of course! One of the master's favorite toys.'

'What about Mr Hoo?' the judge asked again. 'Is he a man of the same ilk as your master?'

Her impassive face suddenly came to life.

'Don't you dare to slander the Honourable Hoo!' she cried. 'He is a fine, straightforward gentleman. A famous hunter and a great warrior, as his forebears were. And now, now he isn't even allowed to wear a sword! That silly ruling is an insult to a man like him.'

'He could have applied for a commission in the Imperial army,' Judge Dee remarked dryly.

'A commission! The heads of the Hoo family were always field-marshals, sir.'

The judge took his fan from his sleeve. The close air in the gallery was becoming oppressive. He fanned himself for a while, then asked abruptly:

'Who killed your master?'

'A newcomer,' she replied at once. 'No one in the

"old world" would have raised his hand against the marquis. Must have been some whore's tout the master let into the house tonight.'

'Has your master had many visitors, lately?'

'No sir. Before the sickness came, the master used to have loose women and their touts here nearly every night. But after some of the servants had died of the sickness, those wretches didn't want to come any more. Mr Mei and Mr Hoo called occasionally. Mr Hoo lives right opposite, across the canal.'

Judge Dee snapped his fan shut. 'By the way,' he asked, 'who was the physician attending upon your mistress?'

'Doctor Lew. A good doctor, they say. But a lecher, of the same sort as the master. He often took part in the parties up here in the gallery. Took part in them up to a point, that is. Everyone knows that Lew can't have a woman.'

'You had better watch that poisonous tongue of yours!' the judge said angrily. 'There's a law on slander. Go and send your son here with a new candle.'

'Very well, sir.'

She went to the door in her ungainly stride.

Judge Dee pensively stroked his moustache.

'Astounding!' he muttered. 'This odd mixture of hate and blind, unquestioning loyalty!'

'It was typical of the time of upheaval, sir, one hundred years ago,' Tao Gan remarked. 'Our empire being then divided into a number of warring states, there was no central authority, no rule of law. For their livelihood, for their very lives, indeed, the people had to rely completely upon their feudal masters. Having a bad master was better than having none—which meant being enslaved by the barbarian invaders, or starving to death.'

The judge nodded. Then he asked, vexedly:

'If Yee was really such a perverted degenerate, why didn't Merchant Mei draw my attention to his doings?'

Tao Gan shrugged.

'Mei was a man of progressive ideas, but he was born and bred in the "old world", sir.'

'And Yee will have taken good care to keep his excesses inside these four walls. In any case, that maid would rather die than give us a clue to his murderer. Her son might tell us more, though. Being so young, he is probably less obsessed by the prejudices of the past. What have you got there?'

Tao Gan had stooped and picked up a small object from the floor, beside the heavy leg of the couch. He showed it to the judge in the palm of his hand: an ear-pendant consisting of a cheap red stone in a simple silver setting. The judge felt the trinket with the tip of his forefinger.

'There's a trace of blood on the fastening hook, not yet quite dried out. There was a woman here tonight, Tao Gan!'

The young doorman came in with a burning candle. While placing it on the table he carefully avoided looking at the dead man.

'Come here!' Judge Dee told him. 'I want to talk to you.'

The youngster's broad, flat face turned a sickly pale. Sweat pearled on his low forehead. The judge concluded that his first impression had been indeed correct: the boy was badly frightened. He asked harshly:

'Who was the woman who came here tonight?'

The boy gave a violent start.

'She . . . she couldn't have done it, sir!' he stammered. 'She was so young, she . . .'

'No, I don't think she murdered your master,' Judge Dee said, in a kind voice now. 'But she may prove an important witness. So you'd better tell all you know about her. For her sake too.'

The youngster swallowed a few times before he replied:

'She came for the first time ten days ago, sir, after the master had sent the servants away. He didn't want my mother or me to see them, he——'

'Them, you say?' the judge interrupted.

'Yes sir. There was a man with her every time. I . . . I spied on them once. Because I had heard her sing, here in the gallery. . . . Such a sweet, beautiful voice!

56

I wanted so much to see what she looked like, so——'

'What about that man?' the judge asked impatiently.

The youngster hesitated. He wiped his face with his sleeve, then he began slowly:

'Well, I couldn't see him clearly, sir, the courtyard being so badly lighted. He was a tout or . . . a bully, I suppose, for he was heavily built, a real giant. And he carried a hand drum. But her I saw clearly, sir. She was very young, and such a sweet, innocent face. Yet she must have danced for the master, for I heard the drum. . . .'

'Did she and her companion come here tonight?'

'I couldn't say sir, really. As I told you already, I was quite busy in the kitchen, helping mother to clean up.'

'All right. You may go.'

As soon as the boy had left, Judge Dee told Tao Gan:

'Those two did come tonight, as proved by the ear-pendant. So that maid Cassia was apparently right when she said it probably was a tout who had killed Yee. The whip suggests that Yee wanted to beat the girl, and the tout would not stand for that. One is wont to despise those men, Tao Gan, and their profession is certainly not a very commendable one. But they too are human beings, and they often have a genuine affection for the women they protect. It is quite possible that the man flew into a rage, wrenched the whip out of Yee's hand, then beat in his head with the iron club those people often carry.'

Tao Gan nodded.

'A strong professional bully would fit the picture all right, sir. It also explains why Yee didn't offer him a chair or a cup of tea.'

'And since they had been here before,' Judge Dee added, 'they knew they could slip outside unnoticed by the small door in the gate that would lock automatically behind them. To locate that dancer shouldn't be too difficult, Tao Gan. She must belong to one of the brothels in the old city.' He paused. Then he doubtfully shook his head and resumed: 'Strange, I had a foreboding that this murder would prove to be uncommonly difficult to solve. . . . And now it turns out to be quite a simple case, after all.' Rising, he added: 'Well, let's search for further clues now. You take the table, the couch and the platform, and I'll have a look at the rest of the gallery.'

He walked over to the portico. The stench of the burnt-out candle still hung in the hot air, so he raised the bamboo curtain of the window on the left, and fastened it with the bands attached to the top. Putting his hands on the broad sill and leaning outside, he discovered that the portico was in fact a kind of balcony, jutting out over the canal, and supported on long, slender pillars rising up from the black water. On the left was a high brick wall, descending into the canal at a slight angle, with a square watchtower at its end. Further along, the low bank was covered with small trees and thick shrubbery. Beyond it he could see the high central arch of the Halfmoon Bridge. To the right the steep outer wall of the mansion terminated in another square watchtower. The canal made a sharp bend there, so the rest of its course was concealed from his view.

He threw a casual look at the two-storeyed house on the opposite bank of the canal, in the bight. So that was the house of Yee's friend Hoo, 'the marshal'! It was built in the elegant style of a country villa, the curved roof-points of its upper storey standing out against the lowering sky. There was a narrow balcony above a row of willow trees; their long branches hung limply down. All the windows were dark. The judge had never had a close look at Hoo's villa while crossing the Halfmoon Bridge, for seen from there it was half concealed by the tall trees that grew on its left. Yet he had the distinct feeling that the details were familiar.

The dank smell of stagnant water and rotting plants made him turn away from the window. Tao Gan was bent over the table, putting together a few porcelain shards. His thin lieutenant looked up and said:

'I think that Yee tried to defend himself, sir. These are the shards of the flower vase. With the rest of the stuff here they tell a fairly clear story—thanks to the sticky ginger syrup, which is a beautiful clue to work with.' When the judge had come up to the table, Tao Gan went on: 'After his visitors had arrived, Yee sat down at the table, and munched a few pieces of ginger. There's syrup on the fingers of his right hand, and a stain on the tip of his sleeve. Then Yee must have taken the whip, for I found syrup on its butt. The murderer became aggressive, and wrenched the whip from Yee's hand, as you suggested already, sir. Or perhaps Yee just let it drop. However that may be, Yee then looked for a weapon to defend himself with, and grabbed the flower vase. As you see from the shards I put together, it was a vase with a long thin neck and a heavy base. But the murderer struck him down before he could use it, for there is no trace of blood on any of the shards. Yee let the vase drop, and it broke to pieces on the floor. We may deduce that Yee grabbed the vase after he had dropped the whip, because two larger shards were lying on top of the thongs of the whip.'

'Good reasoning!' Judge Dee said. 'But how do you know that Yee took the flower vase in his hand? It could have been pushed or have fallen from the table accidentally during the scuffle, couldn't it?'

'Have a look at this shard, sir.'

Tao Gan picked up one larger shard and held it close to the candle. With his thin, bony forefinger he pointed at a brown, sticky smudge. 'This shard formed part of the slender neck of the vase. Why should Yee have grabbed that vase if not to defend himself, sir?'

'Excellent!' the judge said with a pleased smile. 'Ha, that, of course, is what Hoo's villa opposite reminded me of! The Willow Pattern!' He pointed at the dozen or so pieces of porcelain which Tao Gan had neatly fitted together on the table top. They showed the picture of a villa on the waterside, lined by a row of willow trees. The upper storey had a narrow balcony. It had been a good antique piece, the blue design had been painted on in delicate brush strokes.

'All the pieces are there,' Tao Gan said. 'It should

be possible to mend the vase. I looked under the couch, sir, and searched the floor. But without result.'

'Let's walk all along the gallery, and have a look together. Then we must leave, for we have a lot of other work to do, Tao Gan! The search for the dancer and her tout we can leave to the Municipal Tribunal. Here, you take the floorspace in front of the pillars.'

Judge Dee began with the floor of the portico. Suddenly he stooped. A crumpled piece of white cloth was lying against the socle of the third pillar. Squatting down, he called out: 'Bring the candle, Tao Gan!'

Together they examined his find. It was a square piece of thin white cloth, a large handkerchief or scarf. In the center was a red stain.

'That's where the murderer wiped his weapon, sir!' Tao Gan said eagerly. 'Or his hands, perhaps.' He took a piece of oil-paper from his sleeve. 'Here, let me take it up, sir.'

He carried it to the table, and they scrutinized it closely.

'Not a mark, nothing!' Tao Gan said, disappointed.

Judge Dee felt the four corners with his forefinger.

'That's odd,' he said slowly. 'The bloodstain in the middle has nearly dried, but the corners of the cloth feel moist. With water. And look! This is the small leaf of a water-weed sticking to the seam! Wrap this handkerchief up and take it along, Tao Gan. It may be important evidence.' All of a sudden the judge raised his hands and examined them carefully. 'That's very strange!' he exclaimed. 'When I went to open the bamboo roll curtain just now, I noticed that the windowsills in the portico were covered with dust. Later, when leaning out of the left window, I put my hands on the sill. But there isn't a speck of dust on my fingers!'

He quickly stepped up to the left window. Beckoning Tao Gan to hold the candle close, he bent and peered at the red-lacquered surface of the broad sill. 'Thoroughly wiped clean,' he announced. 'And the sills of the other three windows are black with dust.' He turned to the first window and leaned outside; so far that Tao Gan solicitously grabbed his sleeve.

'Look!' Judge Dee cried out. 'A narrow ledge runs along the balcony, just above the pillars that support it. Do you see that green stalk sticking to the edge? That's a water-weed, Tao Gan.' Righting himself he said quietly: 'This means that someone swam across the canal, and entered here by climbing up one of the pillars.'

The judge went to the table, angrily swinging his sleeves. He pulled out the second chair, and sat down heavily. Crossing his arms he looked up somberly and said: 'My foreboding was right, after all, Tao Gan. This is very far indeed from being a simple, straightforward case.'

X

Judge Dee stood at the parapet of the central arch of the Halfmoon Bridge. Resting his elbows on the rough stone surface, he surveyed the dark water of the canal below, lit only by the four large signal lanterns of oil-paper suspended under the arch. Tao Gan, who was standing by his side, slowly wound and unwound the three long hairs that grew from his cheek round his forefinger. They were waiting. The judge had ordered two of the soldiers who had carried their sedan chair to roll Yee's corpse in a reed mat and take it to the Municipal Tribunal for a thorough examination by the coroner. The two other soldiers had been sent away to get another sedan chair, to take the judge and his lieutenant back to the palace.

'What a difference!' Judge Dee spoke up. 'In normal

times this bridge is the hub of city traffic, bristling with activity till far into the night. The parapets are lined with hawkers' stalls with their garish lights, a dense crowd tramps up and down the bridge, and all kinds of large and small vessels, gaily decorated with colored lampions, pass underneath. Now everything is dead and deserted. And do you notice the dank smell? The water in the canal is practically stagnant. Look at those pieces of driftwood, see how slowly they move along!'

'There must be swarms of mosquitoes down there,' Tao Gan remarked. 'Even up here you can hear them buzz. If——'

The judge raised his hand.

'Hush! Is there trouble downtown?'

What had seemed to be the buzzing of mosquitoes was now growing into an indistinct roar. A red glow rose above the houses in the distance.

'The Granary is in that direction,' Tao Gan said worriedly. 'The mob must be attacking it.'

They listened for a long while, in a tense silence. The roar seemed to be dying out, then grew in volume again. Suddenly there was the piercing blast of military trumpets, preternaturally loud over the hushed city.

'Our guardsmen have arrived!' Judge Dee said, relieved. The red glow grew, flames shot up. 'I hope they'll be able to quell the riot without bloodshed,' he muttered. He looked up and down the bridge, but there wasn't a soul in sight. The windows of Hoo's villa remained dark, and nothing stirred in the smaller houses that lined the bank upstream from the bridge. The citizens of the capital, ordinarily so keenly interested in anything unusual happening in the street, had learned to mind strictly their own business, these last three harrowing weeks. The red glow grew faint, and the distant roar died out. All was silent again. A heavy, brooding silence, Judge Dee thought. If the people began to attack the granaries . . .

'The presence of a third man on the scene of the murder certainly complicates matters,' Tao Gan said.

'A third man? Oh yes, the fellow who swam across, you mean.' The judge concentrated his thoughts on the murder, glad of the diversion. 'Well, the swimming bit was easy, of course. But to climb one of those pillars and get onto the ledge of the balcony, that asks for strong muscles. He must have been an acquaintance of Yee, otherwise Yee would have raised an alarm upon seeing a dripping wet man stepping through the window. Did Yee send the woman and her companion away when the third man arrived? Or was he perhaps an ally of the pair? And against whom did Yee want to defend himself with the flower vase? If we assume that——'

The judge broke off. Creasing his bushy eyebrows, he stared fixedly at the dark villa. 'A famous hunter, Cassia said. . . . Could it be possible?'

'Could what be possible, sir?' Tao Gan asked eagerly.

'Well,' Judge Dee began slowly, 'it just occurred to me that perhaps Yee did not grab the flower vase in order to defend himself. The maid described him as a vicious, mean person. What if he broke the vase deliberately, and in order to draw attention to the Willow Pattern? And thus leave a clue pointing to his friend Hoo, in the villa over there that so closely resembles that pattern?'

Tao Gan pensively tugged at his short goatee.

'It doesn't seem impossible,' he agreed. 'On the other hand, I know from my study of the files that the maid spoke the truth when she said that the "old people" form a closely-knit small community, and that none of its members would dream of raising his hand against Yee, their traditional leader. Yet, if Hoo had a very strong motive . . .'

The judge remained silent. He was slowly stroking his sidewhiskers, his eyes on the dark villa. At last he said:

'Since we are here, Tao Gan, we'd better go over there and pay Mr Hoo a surprise visit. I admit that the clue of the Willow Pattern is a very tenuous one. But Hoo will be able to tell us more about Yee at least, so that we can check Cassia's stories. Come along.'

They walked down the bridge. After having followed the main thoroughfare for a short distance, they saw among the tall trees on their right a rustic bamboo gate. The wooden board suspended above it was inscribed with two elegant characters reading 'Willow Abode'. A winding pathway took them to the villa's gatehouse. The door, lacquered red, was decorated with a pattern of willow leaves in gold.

Tao Gan knocked hard with his bony knuckles. He waited, and when no sound came from inside, he picked up a stone and let it rattle on the wood.

'We are in for a long wait, sir,' he said gloomily. 'We'll have to rouse the doorman from his sleep.'

He had hardly finished speaking when the door swung open. A squat man with extraordinarily broad shoulders and long, ape-like arms looked them up and down suspiciously. His greying head was covered by a skullcap. As he raised the candle, the wide sleeve of his houserobe fell back, revealing a hairy, muscular forearm.

'Were you expecting visitors, Mr Hoo?' Judge Dee asked blandly.

The squat man let the light of the candle fall on his face.

'Who the devil are you?' he asked in a deep, rumbling voice.

'I am Dee, the Chief Justice.'

'Holy Heaven! Thousand excuses, my lord! Ought to have recognized you, of course. Saw you only once, however, in full dress, mind you. And from a distance. How——'

'I was just taking a stroll, with my secretary, Mr Tao. Could we have a cup of tea?'

'Certainly, my lord! A great honor, sir! Excuse my dress, but I am all alone in the house, you see. Had to send the servants to the mountains. Infernal nuisance. Kept only an old couple, but they left this afternoon for their son's burial. Promised to be back tonight. But not a sign of them!'

Judge Dee found it difficult to decide whether Hoo's blustering was his natural manner or caused by nervousness. It was a pity he had never met him before.

Or had he? The face seemed familiar, somehow or other.

Talking busily about his household problems Hoo had led them across a neglected inner garden planted with a profusion of wild flowers. Now he made them enter a sparsely furnished reception room, lit by one small oil lamp. The air was close and musty. Hoo made for the table in the rear, but Judge Dee said quickly:

'Couldn't we go upstairs, to a room where I can keep an eye on the bridge? I told my chairbearers to come and fetch me there.'

'Of course! Come up to my study. I was having a nap up there, as a matter of fact. Tea-basket is there too. And a nice balcony.' Taking them up a steep wooden staircase, he added over his shoulder: 'Was awakened by the blast of trumpets. From the direction of the Granary, I'd say. That's the kind of place the rabble makes for, in a time like this. No serious trouble, I hope?'

'Since everything has become quiet again,' the judge replied, 'I suppose it's all right.'

After Hoo had ushered his visitors into a small, square room, he hurriedly pushed open paper-covered sliding doors revealing the narrow balcony the judge had noticed already from the portico of the Yee mansion opposite. Hoo lit with his candle two large, old-fashioned brass candelabra on the wall table, and bade his guests take the two armchairs by the rustic bamboo table in the center of the room. He poured tea, then sat down on a camp-stool, his back to the sliding doors.

Sipping his tea, Judge Dee reflected that the room, scantily furnished as it was had a rather pleasant, much lived-in atmosphere. The broad couch against the side wall was covered with animal skins, and the large wardrobe of ebony dulled by age was a valuable antique. On the back wall hung a good scroll painting, representing an ancient warrior in full battle dress, riding a beautifully caparisoned horse. The picture was flanked by long-bows, quivers, spears and leather harnesses, suspended on iron hooks in the plaster wall.

Hoo had followed Judge Dee's gaze.

'Yes, hunting is my one and only hobby,' he said. 'My great-grandfather used this villa as a hunting lodge, you know. At that time this crowded city quarter was a fine stretch of wooded country.'

'He was a great warrior, I heard,' the judge said.

A pleased grin lit up Hoo's broad face.

'That he was, my lord! Splendid horseman, and a good general. He and the great-grandfathers of Yee and old Mei kept the peace in these parts, in the midst of a free-for-all among the barons and the feudal warlords. Yes, the times have changed, by Heaven! Yee owned the land, my great-grandfather controlled the army, and old Mei had the ready cash. When General Li—excuse me, the August Founder of the Present Dynasty, I should say, of course—when he had reunified the empire, the three old men held council. Historical meeting, my lord, all written up in our family annals. My great-grandfather told them: "Let's call it a day, and cut our losses. Yee applies for a governorship in a distant province, I enlist with my men in the new Imperial army, and Mei sits back and collects his rents." Wise old bird, my ancestor was! But the old Marquis Yee, the stubborn bastard, he wouldn't listen, you see. "Better just lie low for a bit," he said. "Maybe we'll yet get a chance to come back." Fat chance they had! This place was made into the imperial capital, soon it was flooded by thousands of people from outside, court personnel, officials big and small, military, constabulary and what not, and now you have to look damned hard to find uptown a man who even knows the name of Yee!'

He sadly shook his large head.

'What about your own family?' the judge asked.

'We? Oh well, we sold out our land, bit by bit. Now I have only this villa left, and mortgaged to the hilt! But it'll last my time. I have neither chick nor child, and I manage all right. Do a bit of hunting up country, and I drop in on old Yee over there for a drink and a chat. Yee lost all his land, of course, but he is still a rich man. Gay dog, Yee is! Likes to have a couple of nice wenches around and I don't mind that a bit.'

'Quite. It seems that the Mei family was the only one of the three that succeeded in conserving its former assets.'

'The Meis were always damned clever at making money,' Hoo said bitterly. 'Sucked up to the new officials, became pally with the big merchants from the south. That's the way to become a millionaire. Which doesn't prevent you from falling down the stairs and breaking your neck, apparently!'

'Mr Mei's death was a great loss,' Judge Dee said dryly. 'You mentioned Yee's parties just now. Do you happen to know the young dancer he is having up there regularly these days?'

Hoo's face fell.

'Porphyry you mean, eh? So the news has got about already. Yes, I saw the wench there, once or twice. Fine dancer. Sings well, too.'

He did not seem inclined to pursue the subject farther, this time. The judge asked:

'Which brothel does she belong to?'

'Trust Yee to keep that secret, the sly scoundrel! Never let me talk to her or to her tout alone.'

'You mean the tall bully who always accompanies her?'

'Tall bully, you said? Hardly ever gave the chap a second look, but I wouldn't call him that. Elderly fellow, a bit high-shouldered. Damned good drummer, though.'

Judge Dee emptied his cup.

'There was some commotion over there in the Yee mansion tonight,' he said casually. 'Did you notice anything? From the blacony here you have a good view of Yee's gallery.'

Hoo shook his head.

'I was asleep on that couch. When those blasted trumpets woke me up everything was pitch dark over there.'

'The dancer Porphyry was with Yee. There was an accident.'

His host sat up. Laying his large hands on his knees, he asked: 'An accident? What kind of accident?'

'Yee was killed.'

Hoo half rose from his seat.

'Yee dead!' he shouted. As the judge nodded, he sat down again. 'Dead, by Heaven!' he muttered. Suddenly he cast Judge Dee a sharp look and asked tensely: 'Did he lose an eye?'

The judge raised his eyebrows. He considered the question for a moment, then he replied quietly:

'Yes, you might say Yee did. It was his left eye.'

'Holy Heaven!' Hoo's face had turned pale under the tan, his big frame sagged. 'Holy Heaven!' he repeated. Noticing that the judge and Tao Gan were staring at him, he managed a smile and said: 'Shouldn't mind that silly jingle, of course. My head is still on my shoulders!' He passed his hand over his face, which was moist with sweat.

Judge Dee studied him for a brief while, pensively stroking his beard. Hoo had become a changed man.

'There often is more in those street songs than meets the eye, Mr Hoo. Have you any idea who could have wanted to murder Yee?'

'Murder Yee?' Hoo repeated mechanically. 'Well, he did a bit of money-lending, you know. Could become very nasty when the fellows didn't pay up in time. And if you press a man too hard . . .' He shrugged his shoulders.

The judge was struck by the fact that Hoo was not talkative any more. He put his hand in his sleeve and brought out the ear-pendant. Showing it to Hoo, he asked: 'Do you recognize this bauble?'

'Of course. Porphyry wore those. Because of her name, I suppose.' He scratched his beard and added: 'Wouldn't be astonished if the wench had something to do with it. Sweet innocent young thing, she seemed, and still a virgin, they said. An apprentice-courtesan, she called herself. Apprentice, my foot! She hadn't anything to learn any more, not she! Those airs of childlike innocence! The core was rotten, I tell you!' He rubbed his face again, he was sweating profusely. 'Little sweet thing didn't mind dancing stark naked in the gallery! And while doing her niftiest tricks, she'd give me that

68

peculiar look, as if she did it only for me. Made eyes at me all the time, behind Yee's back. And her tout managed to slip me a message from her once, saying that Yee was threatening her, and couldn't I do something about it? Well, I'd certainly have gone a long way to keep her out of that devil's clutches, lewd slut as she was!'

He shrugged and resumed: 'Well, since Yee is dead and gone, and since the line died out with him, there's no harm in telling you, I suppose. Yee's main hobby was maltreating women, sir. It ran in the family. The things his grandfather, the old marquis did, wouldn't make a pretty story. But the times have changed, so Yee had to be careful. Got his way with the sluts from downtown, and mostly from among the "old people". But Porphyry, she was quite different, she had class. Wouldn't he have loved to get her! By Heaven, you should've seen Yee drool when she was dancing, see that mean look in his eyes! But she kept him at a proper distance, the clever little bitch!'

'Did Yee know that you were charmed by the dancer too?'

'Charmed, you say? Funny you hit on just the right word. I am no hand at explaining things, you know, but let's put it this way: every time I saw the wench, she drove me crazy. But when she wasn't there, I'd hardly think of her at all. Believe it or not, but that was the way it was. Did Yee know? He damn well did!' Hoo turned round and pointed at the dark Yee mansion across the water. 'He had thought up a new trick of late, the devil. After this part of the town had become deserted at night. The mean bastard would not warn me when she was coming, but roll up those bamboo curtains, light a lot of candles in the gallery, and make her do her dances in the portico to be sure that I would see it, from the balcony here! By Heaven, he was a mean devil!'

He angrily hit his fist on his knee. After a while Judge Dee asked:

'Were other guests present at those parties in the gallery?'

JUDGE DEE HAS TEA IN THE WILLOW ABODE

'Only Doctor Lew. Always thought doctors didn't go in for those pastimes! But Yee never invited him when Porphyry came. That pleasure he wanted to share only with me, his best friend! For Heaven's sake!' He shifted on his camp-stool, evidently he expected his visitors to leave. But Judge Dee took his folding fan from his sleeve, sat back in his chair, and said, slowly fanning himself:

'I noticed that the architect who built this villa took the well-known porcelain design of the Willow Pattern as model.'

Hoo sat up.

'The Willow Pattern, eh?' he asked slowly. Then, with a determined effort regaining some of his former bluff manner, he said boisterously: 'The other way round, sir; the other way round! It was this villa here that served the pottery chaps as a model.'

Judge Dee exchanged a quick look with Tao Gan.

'I never knew that,' he told his host. 'I heard all kinds of stories about the origin of the pattern. About an old mandarin with a young daughter who . . .'

Hoo cut him short with an impatient gesture.

'All stuff and nonsense, my lord! An old man with a young daughter, forsooth! No, the true story is different. Quite different. But our family never spoke up. The truth does not do much credit to us, you see. Have another cup of tea, my lord!'

While Hoo was refilling their cups, the judge thoughtfully observed him. Hoo's mood had changed again. There had come an inward look into his large eyes, and when he spoke up his voice was quite steady.

'The story goes back to my great-grandfather. To his later years, when the dynasty had been founded, and when he had lost his power. He was still a very wealthy man, though. Lived in grand style, in the family mansion, in the old city. Well, he fell madly in love with a beautiful young wench, in one of the city's brothels. Sapphire, her name was. Love at first sight, that crazy passion of an old man, you know. Bought her for six gold bars; damned expensive, but she was a virgin, you see. He built this villa for her. Since she

71

had that slender waist that our poetry chaps call willow waist, he planted willow trees along the bank, and called the place Willow Abode. You may have noticed the inscription on the gate. That is in his own handwriting.

'Surrounded her with luxury, the old man did. But woman takes a lot of knowing! A young fellow of the Mei clan saw her; they fell in love, and decided to elope together. At that time there was a water pavilion in the moat here—the canal, you call it nowadays—connected with our garden by a narrow wooden bridge. My father had the pavilion pulled down, the pillars were rotting away. Well, on the appointed night, that fellow Mei had moored a fast junk under the pavilion, with a crew of good rowers. He thought the old man was tied up in the city, that day.

'Just when he was helping Sapphire pack her things, up in her room, at the other end of this floor, the old general walked in. He was over sixty then, but still as strong as an ox, and young Mei fled, with the wench on his heels. They ran down into the garden, my enraged ancestor behind them, waving his knobstick. When they were crossing the bridge, the old man gained on them, and he would have killed them both then and there. But the excitement had been too much for him and he suddenly collapsed, unconscious. The couple didn't give the old man a second look. They jumped into the boat, and off they went. Took refuge in the domain of the Marquis of Yeh, our old enemy. Young Mei became his financial adviser, I believe. Damned good money-grubber he was, just like all those Meis.'

Hoo pushed an unruly grey lock away from his sweating brow. He was looking at the darkness outside, with lowering, brooding eyes.

'The old man lived on for six more years, completely paralyzed. Had to be fed with a spoon, like a small child. Sat every day in his armchair on the balcony here, moving only his eyes. They had a strange look, they said, nobody ever knew whether it was love or hate. Whether he wanted to sit there to gloat over the scene where he nearly succeeded in killing her, or be-

72

cause he was still hoping he would see her come back, some day.'

There was a long silence, broken only by Hoo's heavy breathing. He was still staring outside, his hands clenched, deep wrinkles in his broad, low forehead. Now he wiped his face with his sleeve, darted an uneasy look at his two guests from his bloodshot eyes, and said with a sickly grin:

'Please excuse my rambling on, my lord! All this will hardly interest you. Old story, all about people who are dead and gone!'

His voice had become hoarse, and he swallowed hard.

'You never married, Mr Hoo?' the judge asked.

'No sir, I didn't. Families like mine don't belong to this modern world, sir. We have had our day, so why carp? Mei is dead, Yee is dead, and I'll join them in due course.'

Tao Gan gave the judge a sign. He had seen a sedan chair halting on the bridge.

Judge Dee rose. Straightening his robe, he said:

'I am glad I know now the real story of the Willow Pattern, Mr Hoo. And many thanks for the tea!'

Their host silently led them downstairs.

IX

Ma Joong and Chiao Tai were waiting on the marble terrace. Judge Dee cast a quick glance at their drawn faces, smeared with soot. He sat down at the table and asked curtly:

'How is it downtown?'

'All is quiet again, sir,' Ma Joong answered in a

listless voice. 'A mob of about four hundred strong had gathered in front of the Granary. Mostly "old people", judging by their dialect. Fortunately, Brother Chiao and I were inspecting the sewers only one block from there, and we heard their shouting. When we arrived on the square, they were tearing up the pavement and throwing stones at the twenty halberdiers posted in front of the Granary's gate. Twenty archers had taken up position along the battlement above. More than those forty men we hadn't been able to spare, sir. Well, hitting out left and right with the flat of our swords, we forced our way through the crowd to our men at the gate. I tried to make the people see reason, but the ringleaders shouted, "Stone the running dogs of the runaway emperor!" and we couldn't make ourselves heard. Others arrived with burning torches, and they threw those at our men, and on the roof of the Granary.' He stopped because his voice had become so hoarse that he could hardly speak. While he poured himself a cup of tea, Chiao Tai spoke up:

'We first ordered the footsoldiers to form a square and try to drive the mob back with their long halberds. But we saw at once that those twenty would be stoned to death in no time. When a corner of the Granary's roof took fire, we had to order the archers to shoot.' Ma Joong spat out a mouthful of tea over the balus-trade.

'Not a pretty sight, sir,' he said gruffly. 'You know those new-type crossbows. Their iron-staffed arrows go right through an ordinary shield. And they are barbed too. In battle, they are fine weapons to fight with. But to use them on a civilian crowd, that's a sickening business, sir. And there were women among them too. I saw two men speared on one and the same arrow, like roast meat on a spit. Well, after our archers had shot two volleys, first one at those in the rear, then one at those in front, the mob scattered and fled, dragging along their wounded. They left over thirty dead behind.'

'By shooting those thirty men,' Judge Dee said gravely, 'you saved uncounted thousands of citizens from starvation. If the mob had succeeded in plundering and burning the Granary, a few hundred people would have eaten their fill tonight, but that would have been all. If doled out in the regular rations, on the other hand, the stores will supply the population of the entire city with their basic food for at least another month. It was not a pleasant duty, but it couldn't be helped.'

'If old Mr Mei hadn't died we wouldn't have had the riot,' Tao Gan said soberly. 'Mei used to harangue the crowd while distributing free rice in the market, telling them to have patience, because the rain would come soon and wash the city clean of the sickness. And they trusted him.'

The judge lifted his head and looked up at the sky. 'Not a breath of wind in the air,' he said dejectedly. Then he sat up in his chair and resumed in a brisk voice: 'Take a seat! I shall tell you about Yee's murder. It's a strange case that'll help to take your mind off what happened downtown.'

His three lieutenants pulled seats up to the table. After Tao Gan had poured out fresh tea, the judge gave a succinct account of what he and Tao Gan had found in the Yee mansion, and of their conversation with Hoo. He saw to his satisfaction that the taut faces of Ma Joong and Chiao Tai relaxed with their mounting interest in his exposition of the facts. When he had finished, Ma Joong exclaimed:

'Hoo is our man, sir! He had the opportunity, the physique needed for utilizing the opportunity, and a strong motive, namely his jealousy of Yee, who was monopolizing the dancer.'

'And Yee must have smashed the flower vase deliberately, so as to leave a clue to Hoo in his Willow Pattern villa,' Chiao Tai added. 'A broken vase or jug can be a very nasty weapon when used as a club, but only street-roughs are aware of the fact. Certainly not a gentleman-born like Yee. Let's have Hoo arrested, sir!'

Judge Dee shook his head.

'Not so fast! Hoo was doing his best to act the part

75

of the blunt, blustering country squire. But his best wasn't good enough, for the man was laboring under some strong emotional conflict. And I had the distinct impression that the dancer Porphyry was but a minor element in that conflict. That's why he told us all about her and about the way her sensual beauty affected him; without realizing that in doing so he was sticking out his neck for the executioner's sword, so to speak. That, among other things, makes me inclined to give him the benefit of the doubt. For the time being, that is.'

Tao Gan tugged at his thin goatee.

'To tell incriminating half-truths with a great show of sincerity,' he observed, 'is a trick commonly practiced by astute criminals. Another thing that seemed to me suspicious was that Hoo didn't show the slightest interest in the manner of Yee's death.'

'He was very much interested in Yee's eye, though,' Judge Dee said.

'Thought of the street song, eh?' Chiao Tai asked.

'That jingle was indeed worrying him considerably,' the judge said. 'I can't see why it should. Another thing I'd like to know is why Porphyry went out of her way to stir up trouble between Yee and Hoo. Yee is rich and Hoo is poor, so why should she risk losing a good customer by making eyes at Hoo? Oh yes, I forgot to tell you that both Yee's maid and Hoo confirmed our impression that Doctor Lew's private life is very questionable; the man is a lecher. That's why I am not happy to see him hanging about Mrs Mei. She is still a handsome woman, and now that her husband has gone she is quite unprotected. I was a fool to have sent Lew with my message to her. Have a look and see whether the senior scribe is back yet, Tao Gan!'

'Returning to the situation downtown, sir,' Ma Joong began, 'it appears that the scavengers are developing into a real problem. As you know, the wardens had to scrape the bottom of the barrel to get together a sufficient number, and all kinds of vagabonds and crooks joined their ranks. One could hardly pick and choose, for theirs is not a very enviable job, of course. But the fact is that their black hoods serve another purpose besides just protecting them against infection. They ensure anonymity, and many of those scoundrels abuse that for stealing and extorting money from the people whose dead they come to collect.'

Judge Dee hit his fist on the table.

'As if there wasn't enough trouble already! Order the municipal constables to keep an eye on those wretches, Ma Joong. The first one they catch pilfering shall be flogged in the market. And let it be known that, if they commit serious crimes, they shall be beheaded on the spot. We must set a few warning examples, otherwise the situation will get completely out of hand.'

Tao Gan came back, followed by the senior scribe.

'We have drawn up an inventory of all the valuables in the Mei mansion, my lord,' the scribe reported respectfully. 'The housemaster assisted us; he has fortunately completely recovered. We also sealed the safe and the cashboxes pending the arrival of the deceased's cousin. I saw to it that the body was properly dressed and placed in a temporary coffin.'

'Was Doctor Lew there too?'

'Oh yes, my lord. He was a great help in listing the assets. When we left, he was still discussing various houeshold problems with Mrs Mei.'

'Thank you.' After the scribe had taken his leave, the judge said peevishly: 'Just as I thought! I do hope that Mrs Mei will leave for the mountain villa directly after the funeral service.'

'She should have done so three weeks ago,' Tao Gan remarked dryly. 'Mere common sense. I must say that, although Mrs Mei looks and behaves as a lady born, sir, I have my doubts about it. When I was studying the Mei file in the Chancery, I found the record of the marriage, concluded thirteen years ago; it gave no particulars beyond her name, surname and age. I worked through the dossier a second time, but didn't find one word about her or her family. I wouldn't be astonished to learn she was a courtesan, bought out by old Mei.'

Ma Joong and Chiao Tai exchanged an amused look. They knew that Tao Gan was incurably inquisitive, and that being unable to satisfy his curiosity always irritated him beyond measure. Judge Dee smiled. Then he asked, serious again:

'What about those sewers in the old city?'

'All clogged up with dirt and refuse, sir,' Ma Joong replied. 'Swarming with rats. Big, horrible creatures with long, naked tails. Even the biggest cats don't dare to tackle them. I had my men seal the holes off with iron gratings. The wretched people living in the slums told me that the rats often bite off a finger or a toe of a sleeping person. Once they even attacked and killed a baby in its cradle.'

'We must have the sluices that connect the canal with the river opened at once,' the judge said quickly. 'Then the sewers will be swept clean and the rats will leave when the refuse they thrive on is gone. Tao Gan, have this order transmitted at once to the guards at the east and west city gates!' When Tao Gan had left, he asked Ma Joong and Chiao Tai: 'What is your further schedule tonight?'

'We thought of having a brief nap, sir,' Ma Joong answered, 'then going out again, and making the rounds of our military guard-posts. Brother Chiao'll take those uptown, and I'll go downtown. As I told you already, we haven't enough soldiers to man those posts properly, and a few encouraging words will go a long way to cheer up the officers in charge. Our shortage of men really poses a serious problem, sir. As proved by the incident at the Granary. Could you perhaps authorize us to request the commander of the Palace Guard to lend us a hundred footsoldiers or so, sir?'

'Certainly. Tell the senior scribe to write out an order to that effect, then I'll sign and seal it. The Imperial Palace is surrounded by broad moats and high walls, and therefore easy to defend. Moreover, the mob is out for food more than for looting.' He thought for a moment or two, then added: 'When you are in the neighborhood of the Halfmoon Bridge, Ma Joong, I would like you to have a look at Hoo's villa, just on the off-chance that he is having company. When I called on him with Tao Gan, I had the impression that he was expecting a visitor. I don't rule out the possibility that Hoo is in collusion with that dancing girl Porphyry, and she might visit him. This is their chance, for Hoo is all alone in the house. Should she be there, you arrest them both. I have ordered the wardens and the constables to check the brothels for information on that girl, but they have their hands full and I doubt whether they have the time and the men to make a thorough job of it. Well, now the two of you had better retire! Have a wash, and a good nap!' Looking up at Ma Joong, he suddenly asked with concern: 'Did you get hit by a stone, at the Granary?'

Ma Joong fingered the lump on his forehead, grinning a little self-consciously.

'No sir. There was a small scuffle in the Tavern of the Five Blessings where I was waiting for Brother Chiao. I wanted to go to the rescue of a girl who was being bothered by four ruffians. I stumbled and hit my head against a corner of the table. She didn't need my help, as it turned out. She is an expert in fighting with loaded sleeves, you see.'

'That's very interesting,' Judge Dee said. 'I have heard about that art. Is it really as deadly as it is reputed to be?'

'It sure is! The wench had the four fellows on the run before you could say knife. Broke the arm of one of them, too. And she did it all with only one loaded sleeve!'

'I thought they always used two,' the judge remarked. 'Like fighting with two short swords, as practiced also by some of those lowly women.'

'She isn't a lowly woman at all, sir,' Ma Joong said earnestly. 'She is the daughter of a traveling puppeteer. A grumbling kind of chap, but quite well educated.'

'Her twin sister Coral,' Chiao Tai put in, 'happened to be the girl who was bothered by Doctor Lew in the street here, earlier tonight.'

'Her I didn't see,' Ma Joong said indifferently. 'But her sister Bluewhite is a fine, strapping young woman, sir. Quiet and decent girl. Not at all that vulgar and noisy type one so often finds among traveling show-people.'

The judge gave Chiao Tai a questioning glance. During the many years Ma Joong had been in his service, his tall lieutenant had always shown a regrettable but very pronounced preference for vulgar and noisy young women. Chiao Tai answered Judge Dee's look by raising his left eyebrow, his mien expressing immense skepticism.

The judge rose.

'I shall now have a look at things in the Chancery. Come and see me at breakfast tomorrow. Today, I should say, rather. For it's well past midnight!'

XII

After a cat-nap of barely an hour, Ma Joong set out for the old city. It was getting on for two o'clock in the morning. He had exchanged his heavy battledress of mail for a comfortable jacket of brown cotton, and put on his head a flat black cap instead of the cumbersome iron helmet. He had a long walk ahead, and there would not be any trouble about identification, for all the officers in charge of the military posts he had to visit knew him personally.

When he had inspected the fourth post, he found himself in the neighborhood of the Halfmoon Bridge. He decided to have a look at the Hoo villa, as Judge Dee had ordered him.

Having walked up the bridge, he remained standing at the parapet of the central arch for a moment, to orientate himself. The villa was dark except for a faint light behind paper-covered sliding doors on the first floor, where there was a narrow balcony.

'So Hoo has indeed got company!' he said with satisfaction. 'We shall join the festivities!'

A lapping sound from below made him look over the parapet. It was caused by the strong current that swirled around the piers of the bridge, then rushed on in foaming eddies.

'Wish we could open sluices in the sky too,' he muttered, 'to get some movement in this damned stagnant air. We . . .'

Suddenly he broke off. Grasping the edge of the parapet, he leaned over as far as he could. Further downstream, near the left bank, just under the balcony of Hoo's villa, something white glimmered in the dark water. For one brief moment he had a glimpse of a bare arm.

He rushed down the bridge and threw himself into the thick brushwood, well upstream from the drowning person. Thorny bushes scratched his face and hands but he struggled on till he had arrived down at the waterside. The current had eaten deeply into the bank, carrying away large chunks of earth. He kicked off his felt shoes, stepped out of his trousers, and threw those, together with his jacket and cap, into the shrubs higher up the bank. Standing up to his knees in the mud, he steadied himself by grabbing a branch of a half-submerged shrub and peered at the surface, glimmering in the light of the signal lanterns under the bridge. Again he saw an arm rise from the water. The drowning person was struggling desperately, but strangely enough the current did not affect his position. He seemed to be held by an invisible something below the surface.

Ma Joong plunged into the swift stream. After a few strokes he recognized the danger. There was an extensive patch of waterweeds there, a mass of tough stalks and trailers. In the stagnant water they had become solidly rooted in the canal bed, and now even the strong current could not dislodge them. Evidently the drowning person had become entangled with those. Ma Joong had been born and bred in the water-district of

81

Kiangsu Province, and he was in his element here. Knowing that any hurried movement would entangle his arms and legs hopelessly in the long, clinging streamers, he just let himself drift with the current, moving his legs up and down only just enough to prevent them from sinking down, and clearing his way through the waterweeds on the surface with his hands. He could discover no sign of the person in distress. Suddenly, however, his groping hands met long tresses, then a bare arm. He quickly passed his left hand under a soft back and, vigorously striking out with his right, he raised the head above the surface. He looked into the deadly pale face of Bluewhite. Her eyes were half-closed.

'Put your hands on my shoulders and keep still!' he hissed. He saw to his relief that her lips twitched. She began to retch. He let his legs sink down till his feet found a clear space. Treading water, he passed his right hand along her smooth legs and deftly freed them from the tangled trailers. He realized that, tired and out of training as he was, it would be an arduous job to get her safely to land. With a pang of anxiety he saw that her eyes had closed. She had passed out. He reflected that, although this fact would make her easier to handle, he had to hurry to prevent her from dying on his hands, for her bosom didn't seem to move any more. 'I must hurry without hurrying, a devilish job!' he thought, taking a deep breath.

He turned over on his back and put her limp body between his legs, keeping her mouth and nose clear of the surface by cupping his left hand under her chin. His feet caught in a new mass of waterweeds, but he succeeded in freeing himself. He swam with the current, heading for a tree that overhung the bank beyond Hoo's garden.

'Hefty wench!' he grunted as he clambered on land with his burden. He felt about with his foot till he found a clear space among the shrubs where there was long grass. There he stretched her out face down and began to move her arms vigorously. He had to do it all by feel, for here among the tall shrubs it was pitch dark.

She brought up a great deal of water, and he realized with immense relief that she was still alive. When he put his hand on her face he felt her eyelids flutter, and her lips moved. He quickly turned her over on her back. Kneeling by her side he began to massage her cold, stiff limbs. He was panting heavily, and he did not know whether the moisture that gushed down his face and shoulders was canal water or his own sweat.

Suddenly he heard her whisper:

'Keep your hands off me!'

'Shut up!' he gasped. Then, realizing that she could hardly have recognized him, he added more gently: 'I am the soldier who helped you clean your sleeve in the tavern, remember? I had been talking there with your father.'

He thought he heard a faint chuckle.

'You fell flat on your face,' she murmured.

'So I did,' Ma Joong said sourly. 'Planned to help you, but you can take care of yourself. Except tonight. How did you get into the canal?'

Rubbing her thighs he noticed with admiration how firm the solid muscles were.

'I am feeling rotten,' she said softly. 'Tell me first how you happened to discover me. It's hours past midnight already.'

'Well, we are supposed to kind of make the rounds, you see, at night. I was standing on the bridge over there, and spotted you. My name is Ma Joong, by the way.'

'Lucky you saw me. Thank you, Mr Ma.'

'It was all in the day's work. Now, what about you? I don't suppose Mr Hoo chucked you over his balcony, eh?'

'Very funny indeed! As a matter of fact Mr Hoo didn't chuck me over the balcony. I jumped.'

'Jumped? From the bridge?'

She heaved a sigh.

'Since you saved me from drowning, I ought to tell you, I suppose. Well, to cut a long story short, my father used to work for that man Hoo. He left Hoo's service years ago, I never knew why. Hoo told me to

83

MA JOONG SAVES A DROWNING GIRL

come to his house tonight because he had discovered something about my father, he said, something he thought I ought to know. Like a fool I went there. I found out that the dirty rat is a lecher. You can stop rubbing me now, by the way. I am feeling fine. Well, we were all alone in the library up there, and he wanted to have me. We had a kind of wrestling bout. I know a thing or two about the game, but the scoundrel is an old hand, and strong as an ox. Finally, when my jacket and skirt were in tatters I was able to place a kick in his stomach that made him reel back. I ran to the balcony and jumped into the river. I am not a bad swimmer, but I hadn't reckoned with those damned weeds.'

'The son of a dog!' Ma Joong exploded. 'As soon as you are feeling all right, we'll pay him a courtesy call, and I'll beat a full confession out of him.'

Suddenly he felt her hand on his breast.

'Don't do that, please!' she said urgently. 'He could ruin my father, you know.' Then she added in a bitter voice: 'Besides, there were no witnesses. Who would believe my word against that of an important man like Hoo?'

'I!' he said promptly. 'Anywhere, any time.'

He felt her arms round his neck. She pulled his head down and kissed him full on his mouth, pressing her bare bosom against his broad chest. He folded her in his muscular arms.

There was none of the hesitant exploration that marks a first embrace. The complete darkness allowed unreserved yielding to passion, yet created an infinite tenderness. When at last he lay down in the grass, one arm still round her shoulders, the other on her heaving bosom, he thought exultantly that he had never before possessed a more delightful woman. They remained lying there side by side for a long time. Ma Joong wished this could last for ever.

Her first words, however, dampened his elated mood.

'It had to happen anyway sooner or later,' she said casually. 'Besides, on an eventful night like this, one more accident doesn't matter.'

85

He was so taken aback that he didn't know what to say. Suddenly she resumed:

'Now, what about clothes? Those mosquitoes are the meanest creatures.'

'I'll go have a look at Hoo's backyard,' he muttered.

'That damned darkness!' he grumbled as he made his way through the shrubs. 'Wish I could've seen her face! Was it her idea of a joke, or did it really mean absolutely nothing to her? Ow!' The stubbly ground and sharp stones were hurting his bare feet.

He climbed over the wooden garden fence, and found a washing line with a few pieces of clothing the servants had apparently forgotten to take inside. He took a patched jacket and a pair of blue trousers.

Handing her the jacket, he said:

'I don't know whether it'll fit you, but it has nice long sleeves for putting those iron thingummies in. Didn't you have them with you tonight?'

'No. I told you I was a fool, didn't I? Thought that a man like Hoo had enough women available to last him for the rest of his life. Didn't you get any shoes?'

'I'll carry you to the place where I left mine.'

Disregarding her protests he took her in his arms and walked off. She was not exactly a light burden, but her cheek against his was adequate compensation for his labor. He set her down by the side of the road, then went to retrieve his belongings. He still had the woodman's instinct acquired during his long years in the 'green forest', so that he found the spot without difficulty. After he had rejoined her, he tore his neck-cloth in two, and stuffed the pieces in his shoes.

'Here,' he said. 'You won't skip about in those like a young doe, but they'll at least protect your dainty feet. Where do you live?'

'Not too far from here, in the quarter behind the Taoist Temple.'

After that they walked along, in a rather awkward silence. Ma Joong looked askance at her a few times, but he could not distinguish her face in the dim light, and he hesitated to reopen the conversation. When

86

they had left the Halfmoon Bridge behind them, however, he began diffidently:

'I'd like to meet you again, you know. Perhaps in . . .'

She halted in her steps. Her arms akimbo, she gave him a scornful look.

'If you think this is the beginning of an easy and cheap love affair, Mister Colonel, I must disillusion you. You saved my life, and I paid cash. That's all there is to it, understand?'

While Ma Joong, deeply hurt, was groping for an answer, she went on bitterly:

'My father is right. All of you high-ups think that every woman of the common people is fair game. Don't your wife and concubines keep you sufficiently busy, my friend?'

'I am not married!' Ma Joong exclaimed, indignant.

'You are lying, of course. As if a man of your rank wouldn't have established a family years ago!'

'I haven't. I shan't pretend that I have been exactly idle in that line all those years, but I didn't marry. There are a few wenches around who kindly hold my hand when I'm feeling lonely, but I keep no regular mistress. Never met the right girl, I suppose.'

'That's what they all say,' she remarked coldly.

'Well, have it your own way, then,' Ma Joong said wearily. 'Let's walk on. I have other work to do tonight besides seeing stray girls home.'

'Yes, Mister Colonel.'

'Don't keep harping on my rank, you stupid wench!' he burst out. 'I don't belong to the upper set that produces nothing but colonels and generals. I am the son of a boatman and damned proud of it too. I am from Foo-ling, a small fishing village in Kiangsu. Means nothing of course to a silly stuck-up city miss like you.' He shrugged, and lapsed into a moody silence. When she said nothing, and made no move to walk on, he pensively scratched his chin and resumed:

'My father was a damned fine fellow. Carried a bale of rice under each arm like a sack of feathers. But the

87

boat was all we had, and when my father died I had to sell it to pay my debts.'

He fell silent. After a while she said quietly:

'I know all about being in debt. What did you do then?'

He looked up, startled from his thoughts.

'Well, I had always done a lot of boxing and fencing, you see, so the local magistrate hired me as his body-guard. He paid well, but he was a mean bastard. Did a dirty trick to a widow once, and I knocked him down. A beauty, straight to his jaw!' He grinned, then gave her a sour look and continued gruffly: 'Hitting a magistrate being a capital offense, I fled and took to the "green woods". Became a highwayman, in case you don't know.'

'I do know. Being a highwayman, how could you become a colonel of the Imperial guards?'

'Because I met my present boss, who happens to be the greatest gentleman alive. He made me his lieutnant, and I have served him the last fifteen years. My career, my rank, everything I owe to him.'

She gave him a thoughtful look.

'Are you really from Foo-ling?' she asked, in the local dialect.

'I'll be damned!' Ma Joong shouted. 'You don't mean to say you are from there?'

'My mother was, originally. She was a sweet woman, but she died some years ago.' She was silent for a while, then added: 'My father belongs to the "old people".'

'He tripped me up, but I think he's a nice fellow nevertheless. Bit of a grumbler, though.'

'He is a great artist,' she said earnestly. 'There was a terrible tragedy in his life, and that has made him bitter.'

They walked on. Soon the green-tiled roof of the Taoist Temple loomed up in front of them. The large paper lanterns hanging from the eaves of the gate-house were still burning.

She laid her hand on his arm.

'Here we'll say good-bye. My father must not know

anything about my visit to Hoo, mind you. I'll tell him that I fell into the canal accidentally.'

Now that he could see her face clearly by the light of the large lanterns, he thought he discerned in her eyes a soft glint that gave him new courage.

'I'd be very glad if we could meet again,' he said. 'Not because of you know what, but just to get to know each other better. Couldn't we get together, somewhere?'

She patted her wet hair.

'Well, if you care to come to the Tavern of the Five Blessings, say tomorrow at noon, I'll try to be there, and we can have a bowl of noodles together. As an acrobat I am considered a social outcast, which has the advantage that I can show myself in public with any man I like. If you don't mind being seen with me, that is.'

'What do you take me for? I'll be there . . . Miss Acrobat!'

XIII

Early in the morning, just after daybreak, Judge Dee walked out on the marble terrace, still clad in his night-robe. One look at the thick, impenetrable wall of yellow fog that surrounded the terrace on all three sides sufficed. This same fog had greeted him every morning for the last three weeks. It meant that there was no breeze, no change of weather and hence no chance of rain. The stricken city was facing one more suffocating day, in a hot, pestilence-laden air.

He went back inside, and pulled the terrace door shut behind him. It was hot in the large, low-ceilinged room, but he had to keep the unhealthy fog outside. Normally this room, located on the top storey of the Governor's palace, was used as banquet hall for smaller parties in summer, when the guests could enjoy the evening cool out on the marble terrace. After the emergency had been declared, and the Grand Council assigned the palace of the Metropolitan Governor to Judge Dee, the judge had decided to make this room his private headquarters. He had the four banquet tables arranged so as to form a square, and placed his own writing-desk in its center. On the first table were put all dossiers and documents relating to the routine city administration, on the second those concerning the emergency measures, on the next the papers of the High Court, while the fourth table was littered with files and folders on the food supply. Thus he had all these documents within easy reach when he sat working at his desk.

Against the back wall stood a couch and a tea table with four chairs, in the corner a simple wash-stand. Judge Dee had lived, eaten, slept and worked here, ever since he had sent his three wives and his children to the mountain villa of one of his friends and locked up his own official residence, to the south of the Imperial palace.

It was from this room that he directed the administration of the city which the Emperor had personally entrusted to him, three weeks before. Then the Emperor, the Court, the Cabinet and all national government organizations had moved to the Imperial Camp in the cool mountain plain, thirty miles from the capital. There a temporary city of tents and barracks had been constructed, and this was now the administrative center of the huge Chinese empire. The capital, its teeming population reduced to two-thirds of the normal figure, had become an island, as it were, isolated by the Black Death that walked its streets. It was left to Judge Dee to see this city of fear through the present emergency.

In Judge Dee's improvised headquarters scores of clerks and orderlies maintained liaison between him and the more important branches of the city government he had installed in the palace. The military administration, headed jointly by Ma Joong and Chiao Tai, was located on the third floor below; the archives, assigned to Tao Gan, on the second floor, while the Municipal Chancery took up the entire ground floor of the palace, as in normal times.

An orderly came in and placed a bowl of rice and a platter of salted fish and vegetables on the tea table. Judge Dee sat down. But after he had lifted his chopsticks he realized that he had no appetite at all. He had been drafting official documents and proclamations with Tao Gan till long after midnight. The two hours of sleep thereafter had been disturbed by bad dreams, a fitful slumber that had left him more tired than before. His throat was sore, and he greedily drank the cup of strong, hot tea. While he was sipping his second cup, Chiao Tai came in. After he had wished the judge a good morning, he poured himself a cup too, and said:

'Everything was quiet uptown, sir. There was only one major crime, just about an hour ago. A sordid affair. Four scavengers who had been called to the house of a captain who had died of the plague, violated the widow and her two daughters. Fortunately their cries attracted the attention of a patrol that was passing by, and the scoundrels were arrested. In accordance with your instructions, sir, I had the military police take them at once to the square of the communal pyre, where most of the scavengers gather. There they were beheaded, with black hoods and all.'

Judge Dee nodded.

'I trust this will serve as a warning. How many of those scavengers are there at present?'

'About three thousand are registered with the municipality, sir. Numbered identification tags are issued to them, and on showing those they are paid their salary every week. It must be feared, however, that many scoundrels joined their ranks, just by putting on a black cloak and hood; not for the salary, but for pilfering and committing other offenses unpunished.'

The judge set down his teacup hard.

'We need inspectors to check them,' he said. 'But no one likes to go near those men, and with our shortage of manpower . . .'

The door opened and Ma Joong came in, followed by Tao Gan.

'I have news about Hoo, sir!' Ma Joong announced with a happy grin. He sat down and told the judge about his night's adventure.

'Astonishing story!' Judge Dee evclaimed. 'Evidently it was she whom Hoo was expecting when you, Tao Gan, and I paid him our surprise visit last night.' He gave Ma Joong a keen look and asked: 'Are you quite sure her story was on the level?'

'You don't think she jumped stark naked into the canal for a nice healthy swim, sir?' Ma Joong asked indignantly.

'Hardly that,' the judge admitted. He thought for a moment or two, then resumed: 'That girl must tell us more about Hoo's relations with her father. Do you know where to find them?'

Ma Joong looked embarrassed.

'Somewhere behind the Taoist temple, sir. But I shall meet her at noon, tomorrow.'

Judge Dee shot him a shrewd look. 'I see,' he said. 'Well, after that meeting you bring her here. Together with her father. In any case, we have now a definite charge against Hoo, namely the capital one of attempted rape. And that comes in very handy.' He went over to his desk and selected an official form. He filled it out rapidly with his red writing-brush. Impressing the large red seal of the High Court on it, he told his three lieutenants: 'With Hoo safely under lock and key, we shall collect more evidence about Yee's murderer.' He clapped his hands.

He gave the warrant to the orderly who came in, and said:

'Hand this to a captain of the guard at once, and tell him to effect the arrest with four men. Hoo may put up resistance, but I want him alive, and with a whole skin, mind you!'

The orderly saluted smartly. Rushing out, he nearly collided with the senior scribe, who told the judge:

'A Mr Fang asks for an audience, my lord. He belongs to the, ah . . . Special Services of the municipality.'

Tao Gan bent over to the judge and whispered:

'He is the chief of the section charged with the supervision of brothels and gambling houses, sir. Good man, I hear.'

'Show him in!' Judge Dee ordered.

A small, wiry man entered, clad in a simple blue gown and wearing a round skullcap. At first sight one would take him for a shopkeeper, but one glance at his face belied that impression. Deep lines divided it as it were into segments. The left eye opened and shut continually through a tic of the drooping eyelid, the other had a cold, unwavering stare. He reminded the judge forcibly of a lizard. He made to kneel, but the judge said impatiently:

'Skip the formalities, and state your business!'

'My office received orders to make a search for a dancer called Porphyry, my lord,' the small man began quietly. 'Since brothels and gambling houses do little business in this emergency, I decided to take the matter in hand personally, and devoted all night to it. I had a talk with the secretary of the Brothel-keepers' Guild and with some of its leading members, while my secret agents questioned the stool pigeons we maintain all over the licensed quarters. The result may be summed up as follows. In the first place, it is out of the question that the girl is an apprentice. Apprentices are allowed to work outside the quarter only when accompanying a full-fledged courtesan, to assist her changing dress, serve wine to the guests, and to sing or play a musical instrument. They are not allowed to dance in public before they have passed their examination, and certainly not lascivious dances performed in the nude; for that is the privilege of a special class of courtesans, who receive an extra allowance. Second, the name Porphyry does not appear on any official or unofficial list. Third, none of the brothels or houses of assignation has received during the past two weeks any order from the late Mr Yee, despite the fact that before that he had been a most regular customer.'

Fixing the judge with his one unblinking eye, the small man resumed:

'My conclusion is, my lord, that the said girl and the man acting as her tout are imposters. The secretary of the guild was highly incensed at this fraud. He passed the word around and put up a reward at once. I expect they will be found very soon.' It was difficult to know whether he winked with his left eye or whether it was just the tic when he concluded in his dry voice: 'The guild council and its members don't take kindly to poaching on their preserve.'

'Thank you,' the judge said. 'This is most useful information.' He wanted to dismiss the lizard-like man, but Tao Gan bent over and whispered something in his ear. After some hesitation, the judge cleared his throat and asked:

'You are accustomed to handle confidential matters, aren't you, Mr Fang?'

'That's why I could keep my post for twenty years, my lord,' the small man replied with a thin smile.

'The fact is,' Judge Dee resumed, 'that I would like you to gather, with the utmost discretion, data about the antecedents of Mrs Mei, the widow of my valued friend Merchant Mei. It has been suggested that originally she was a courtesan.'

'It so happens, my lord, that I can supply that information right away. The little I have, that is. No, she was not a real courtesan. An apprentice, rather. She was registered under the professional name of Sapphire. In a brothel of the old city, thirteen years ago.'

'Did Mr Mei redeem her?'

'He did not, my lord. She just went to live with him.' Seeing that Judge Dee raised his eyebrows, he continued hurriedly: 'I am very sorry, my lord, but this is one of the very few cases within my jurisdiction which I could never solve satisfactorily. I found myself up against two barriers which are particularly difficult to surmount. In the first place, the brothel she worked

94

in belonged to the "old world"—and I have standing orders to leave that milieu alone as long as no crimes are committed there. Moreover, the brothel burned down shortly after, and the keeper and most of the inmates perished in the flames. She was bought out, but I could not discover by whom. Second, the man she went to subsequently was Merchant Mei. Although he was a progressive member of the old set, he would yet become remarkably reticent when their particular problems were brought up. On top of that, he was the wealthiest merchant of the capital, not the kind of person to brook snooping into his private life. That's why I remember the case so well, my lord. Because it is one of the very few that remain open in my books.'

'I don't doubt that,' the judge said. 'I have full confidence in your ability, Mr Fang. Let me know at once when the pseudo-courtesan Porphyry has been traced.'

When the door had closed behind Fang, Judge Dee exclaimed angrily:

'Hoo told us a pack of lies! If I hadn't that earpendant, I would believe that the dancer and her companion never existed except in the imagination of Hoo and the maid. I am all the more glad that I issued that warrant for Hoo's arrest, for . . .' He looked around at the orderly and asked, annoyed: 'What is it now?'

'A messenger from the municipal tribunal reports that Mrs Yee has hanged herself, my lord. Doctor Lew discovered her. The constables . . .'

'I shall deal with the case personally,' the judge told him curtly. He rose and said to his lieutenants: 'What next, I wonder! And Doctor Lew found her! That suave philanderer again. What is my schedule for this morning, Tao Gan?'

'In an hour's time you have to preside at a council of the wardens, sir, to devise means for persuading the farmers to continue bringing their vegetables to the city. Thereafter you will have to receive . . .'

'All right all right! We have an hour to see what happened at Yee's. Get me my robe and cap, we shall go there at once. The four of us.'

XIV

A large military sedan chair carried Judge Dee and his three lieutenants to the Yee mansion. The coroner and his assistant followed in a second chair. The fog had lifted to make place for a thin haze laden with humidity; the empty streets seemed to quiver in the hot air.

It was Doctor Lew who opened the small door in the iron gate. He stared in consternation at the judge.

'I . . . I had expected an officer of the municipality, my lord. I . . .'

'I decided to take the case myself,' Judge Dee told him curtly. 'Lead the way.'

Doctor Lew made a very low bow. They passed the same courtyards as on their previous visit. Arrived at the walled-in garden, however, the doctor did not take them to the gold-paneled door but to a side room which apparently had served as Mrs Yee's boudoir. After a quick glance at the elegant furniture of rosewood, the judge went straight to the couch where the still body was lying, covered by a white piece of cloth. Judge Dee folded back the top. One look at the distorted face with the protruding, swollen tongue sufficed. He motioned the coroner and his assistant to set to work. Having bestowed a pensive look on the maid, who was crouching on the floor in the corner, sobbing convulsively, he decided to question her later. He turned round and went outside, followed by Doctor Lew. His three lieutenants were standing about the small lotus pond. The judge sat down on the rustic seat there and asked Lew:

'When did you find her?'

'Only half an hour ago, my lord. I had come to inquire after Madame Yee's health. Her husband's murder had been a severe shock, of course, and I feared——'

'Never mind that. Come to the point!'

The doctor gave him a pained look. He resumed in a resigned voice:

'The maid Cassia took me straight to the boudoir. She said she was glad I had called, for her mistress had not answered when she knocked on the door to bring her morning tea, and the door had been locked on the inside. Madame Yee's locking herself in always meant that she had had a bad night and was in a depressed mood. I said I would give her a palliative, knocked on the door, and called out that it was I who had come to see her. When I had repeated this several times without eliciting any response, I feared that she had become unwell during the night and would need immediate attention. I asked the maid to call her son, and he broke the lock with a hatchet.'

The doctor fingered his thin goatee and shook his head.

'She was hanging from the central rafter, my lord. We cut the cord at once, but her body was already stiff and cold. It appears that she had pushed the toilet table to the center of the room, and, since an overturned chair was lying on the floor, she must have put that on top of the table, climbed on it, put the noose around her neck and kicked the chair away. I found that her neck was broken so she must have died at once. As her attending physician, my lord, I would suggest a verdict of suicide during temporary insanity.'

'Thank you. You will now join the coroner. Perhaps he will want to ask you some questions.' When Doctor Lew had gone inside again, Judge Dee told his three lieutenants: 'While they are busy here, we shall have a look around. First, the gallery. In broad daylight we may discover clues we overlooked last night. Where's that doorman?' He clapped his hands. As no one appeared, he said: 'Oh well, I think I remember the way.'

JUDGE DEE IN THE BOUDOIR OF A DEAD LADY

He took them through the empty corridors and, after but one wrong turn, found the steps that led up to the gallery. Judge Dee went in first, followed by Tao Gan. Seeing that all the roll curtains were down, he told Tao Gan:

'Better roll those——'

He was interrupted by a loud exclamation behind him. It was Ma Joong. He stood stock-still, staring dumbfounded at the gallery.

'What's wrong with you?' Chiao Tai asked testily.

'This gallery is exactly the same as I saw in Yuan's peep-show!' Ma Joong exclaimed. 'The scene of the man in black whipping a woman!' He pointed excitedly at the portico. 'Only the couch had been pushed over there, in the center. She was strapped to it face down, and——'

'What are you talking about?' the judge asked, astonished. 'Who is Yuan?'

Ma Joong pushed his helmet back and scratched his head.

'It's quite a story——' he began.

'In that case we shall sit down,' Judge Dee interrupted him. 'First roll those curtains up, Tao Gan. I don't like that musty smell in here.'

When they were seated on the couch, Ma Joong gave a detailed account of the puppeteer and his peepshow. 'Finally,' he said, 'Yuan showed me a second scene, of a villa on the waterside. I saw that scene only briefly, for then the candle in the box went out. And last night, when I was standing on the bridge, it was too dark to see Hoo's villa clearly. But now I recognize it all right.' Pointing at the window, he added: 'The second scene Yuan showed me was a picture of Hoo's villa over there.'

The judge looked around at the window, pensively tugging at his moustache. Then he told Ma Joong gravely:

'This can only mean that Yuan knows about Yee's whipping the bondmaid to death here in this gallery six years ago, and that Hoo was also involved in that despicable crime. Since his daughter told you that her

99

father had been in Hoo's service, Yuan may even have been an eye witness. You must get hold of that puppeteer, Ma Joong. I must have a talk with him.'

'I shall do my best, sir!' Ma Joong said with a pleased grin.

Judge Dee got up.

'I would like you and Chiao Tai to have a look at the balcony. Tell me whether I am correct in assuming that only a trained athlete could manage to climb onto it.'

The two friends went to the windows, and the judge and Tao Gan began to walk up and down the gallery, taking in all its unusual features again.

Ma Joong held a brief consultation with Chiao Tai. They stepped up to the judge.

'Shinning up one of those pillars,' Chiao Tai said, 'that wasn't much of a job, sir. But to get up to the ledge is quite a different proposition. You'll have noticed that the ledge sticks out a foot or so over the pillars, then there's three feet again from the ledge up to the windowsill, and nothing to get a hold on. To get inside that way asks for strength and skill. A hunter, accustomed to climbing difficult trees, could manage it all right. But he would have to be a tall fellow too.'

'Hoo isn't tall,' the judge said pensively. 'But I noticed that he has long, ape-like arms. Therefore I would——'

Tao Gan was tugging at his sleeve.

'I overlooked something, sir, last night!' the thin man said ruefully. He pointed at the wainscoting. One of the panels had swung open, just beside the couch.

'It isn't even a secret door,' Tao Gan resumed. 'It has quite an ordinary knob. But those panels all look alike, and since the light was bad . . .'

'Never mind,' Judge Dee said. 'Let's have a look inside!'

It was a rather small room, without any window. The stale smell of cosmetics hung in the close air. Half of the space was taken up by a dressing-table with a large round mirror of polished silver. Apart from that there was only a tabouret and two high clothes-racks. In the back wall was another narrow door.

The judge pulled out the drawers of the dressing-table but found them completely empty. Suddenly he picked up a small object that had become stuck in a fissure of the wood.

'Well well,' he said to the others, 'look at this! That girl Porphyry was in an awful hurry. This is the red stone that belongs to her other ear-pendant.' He put it in his sleeve. 'Now, let's see where that door leads to.'

Ma Joong opened it. They saw a steep flight of narrow steps, which proved to lead down to a long passage without any windows. The small door at the end gave access to the front courtyard of the mansion.

'Yee used this as a shcrt cut to the gallery,' Tao Gan observed. 'Thus he could lead his visitors of questionable morals up there without the servants seeing them.'

'And that stuffy little room was the dressing-room of the wenches. Undressing room, mainly!' Ma Joong remarked.

Judge Dee did not seem to have heard him. He was staring fixedly at the young doorman, who was crossing the yard, carrying a bucket and a broom. When he saw them he made an awkward bow, then scurried away. The judge turned around to Tao Gan and asked:

'Doesn't that youngster's face remind you of someone?'

Tao Gan shook his head, bewildered.

'He has Hoo's traits,' Judge Dee said firmly. 'That's why when I saw Hoo I thought his face looked familiar. Now that I have seen the boy in broad daylight, I am quite sure. You yourself mentioned the loose morals of the old set, Tao Gan. The boy is Hoo's bastard. That gave Cassia, beside her hatred for Yee, a second reason for trying to confuse the issue! It was she of course who wiped the windowsill clean, after she had discovered her master's dead body up in the gallery. In order to obliterate the traces of Hoo's presence.'

He paused, and reflected a long time, slowly combing his long beard with his fingers. The three men watched him intently. Lost in thought, he seemed to have forgotten their presence. At last he looked up and asked Ma Joong:

'To come back to your meeting in the tavern, did the puppeteer know who you were?'

'No sir. He took me for a common soldier. I had taken off my badge, and in battledress officers and men look pretty much the same to an outsider.' He frowned, and added: 'That was before he did his trick with the peepshow, though. After he had shown me that horrible scene, I told him I was a colonel of the guard, because I wanted Yuan to take me to the house behind the tavern to arrest the bastard.'

'I see. That being the case, I have to see that puppeteer right now. Tomorrow will be too late. A pity his daughter didn't give you their address, Ma Joong. Wouldn't the keeper of the tavern know it?'

'He doesn't, sir. I asked him, but he said they have no fixed place to stay. It's a traveling show, sir, after all.'

'All right. As soon as we are through here, you go with Chiao Tai to the quarter behind the Taoist temple, and find them. You bring Yuan to my office, together with his daughter Coral. I don't need her sister. Come along! The coroner'll have finished, by now.'

He turned around on his heel and crossed the court-yard, his arms folded in his wide sleeves.

Doctor Lew and the coroner were waiting in the walled-in garden, seated on the stone seats by the lotus pond. They rose quickly when they saw the judge. The coroner handed him an official form and said:

'I have thoroughly examined the body, sir. She must have done it an hour or so after midnight, the time when the human spirit is at its lowest ebb. There were no signs of violence. I agree with the doctor that she did it in the manner reconstructed by him. I have noted all the details on this form. With your permission, sir, I shall now draw up the death certificate, then have the body placed in a temporary coffin. The maid has given me the address of an old uncle in the east quarter who is the next of kin. I shall have him informed, and he shall come and take charge here.'

Judge Dee nodded. 'Leave two soldiers on guard here,' he ordered. 'I want to have a word with you, doctor. Let's go to the front hall. Ma Joong and Chiao Tai, you two may leave now and see about the matter I mentioned. Tao Gan, you had better go back to the office, and make the papers for the conference of the wardens ready. I shall join you there as soon as I have talked with the doctor here.'

The judge found a small tea table in a corner of the front hall. Wiping the dust off the chair with the tip of his sleeve, he sat down. Motioning Doctor Lew to be seated too, he began affably:

'I am very interested to hear your opinion on Mrs Yee's suicide, doctor. What was her motive, do you think?'

Dr Lew was visibly relieved at this opening. He had evidently been expecting a severe cross-examination. He stroked his goatee and said ponderously:

'It is not always easy, my lord, to establish the correct diagnosis in mental cases. Since I attended upon Mrs Yee regularly, however, I think I might try to formulate an opinion.' He cleared his throat, and continued: 'One should not speak ill of the dead, of course, but it is my duty to inform you, my lord, that Mr Yee was a hard and cruel man, tormented by perverted lusts. He led a highly irregular dissipated life. Mrs Yee loved her husband, and she suffered deeply when she saw him sinking lower and lower. She then sought to escape from her sorrow by telling herself that her husband was a great and good man, and in course of time she ended up by genuinely believing in this wholly artificial image. This fiction gave her the mental rest her precariously balanced mind so desperately needed. When she heard that he was dead, the artificial image suddenly collapsed, and she was faced with the full extent of her self-deceit. That cruel shock was too much for her.'

Judge Dee nodded slowly. Lew had reproduced exactly his own opinion. He was a shrewd fellow who would have to be handled carefully.

'You are an excellent judge of your fellow-men, doctor. Permit me to ask your opinion on another problem. Not a medical one, this time! As a doctor, you hear of course many things that people, and especially the so-called "old people", never tell to outsiders. Now I was told that Mrs Mei's antecedents are somewhat of a mystery. And my chancery staff doesn't like mysteries when they have to draw up official documents relating to an inheritance. A large inheritance. I wonder whether you could enlighten me.'

Dr Lew seemed taken aback. When the judge met his questioning look blankly, he said with a thin smile:

'The mystery you refer to was deliberately created, my lord. I shall tell you the secret, in the strictest confidence, of course. It came to my knowledge in an . . . ah, professional manner.'

'Do you mean the fact that Mrs Mei was a former courtesan?'

'Oh no, my lord! Yes, that, of course, is the risk one takes if one wilfully creates mysteries! People love scandal, and irresponsible persons will spread all kinds of nonsense! No, my lord, Mrs Mei never was a courtesan. On the contrary, she belonged to a very distinguished family, in the old city here.'

'Why the mystery, then?'

'Because there existed an old feud between her father's family and the Mei-clan, my lord. Her father strongly opposed the marriage. But, although Mr Mei was twice her age, she recognized his great qualities, and she persevered. When her father kept refusing, she eloped and just went to stay with Mei, and the marriage was concluded privately, later. A remarkable woman, my lord! Her father was in a towering rage, but he could do nothing about it, and he left for the south. That is all, my lord.'

'Astounding how people will gossip! Well, I shall tell my staff that everything is in order. Have you any suggestions as to how we could further diminish the risk of infection among the population, doctor?'

Dr Lew gave a lengthy medical exposition to which the judge listened attentively. Despite his weakness for women, the man was certainly a learned physician.

Judge Dee thanked him warmly, and the doctor led him to the main gate, where the military sedan chair was waiting.

XV

Ma Joong and Chiao Tai stared sourly at the two Taoist monks that were again making a low bow, their long yellow sleeves sweeping the floor. The four men were standing at the head of the broad stone steps leading up to the high gatehouse of the Taoist temple.

Two hooded men came walking down the street. One of them lifted the rim of his black hood and shouted up at the monks in a raucous voice:

'Our amulets sell better than yours, stupid quacks!'

The other guffawed. It echoed loudly in the empty street.

'Of those insolent rogues we have enough and to spare, in this quarter,' the eldest monk told Chiao Tai. 'But we have never seen a puppeteer around here.'

'Nobody has visited our temple anyway, these last ten days,' the other monk remarked. 'We just pray for rain, all day and all night.'

'Keep on praying!' Ma Joong said ungraciously. 'Good-bye!'

He gave a sign to his friend and they went down into the street.

Chiao Tai cast a dejected look at the row of shops opposite. All the shutters were closed.

'Apparently they open up for only one hour in the early morning,' he remarked, 'just like those uptown. Sell out the little foodstuffs they have, and close again. Who the hell is there to ask about that puppeteer and that girl of yours? We can't knock on every damned door in this quarter, can we?'

'It won't be easy,' Ma Joong admitted gloomily. 'There isn't even a single street urchin about. They would know, of course, for they are fond of puppet shows. In normal times.'

Chiao Tai had been plucking at his small black moustache. Suddenly he asked:

'What did that small monkey of Yuan's look like exactly? The light in the tavern was so bad that I couldn't see it well.'

'Yuan's monkey? What do you want with that?'

'Did it have a tail?'

'It did. Long, furry affair. Curled it round Yuan's neck.'

'Good! That means it's a tree monkey!' Chiao Tai exclaimed.

'So it's a tree monkey. What is so good about that?' Ma Joong asked peevishly.

Chiao Tai was looking up at the temple with a speculative eye.

'I think, brother,' he said pensively, 'that we'd better go and climb that pagoda over there.'

'What for? You need exercise?'

'To look for trees, brother. There can't be many around, for in this poor quarter people can't afford the luxury of a garden. Now itinerant artists who keep monkeys that go around among the audience with the collection-plate always treat them well, for those trained monkeys are worth a lot to them. So that fellow Yuan will have tried to find a lodging where there's a tree of some sort, to keep his monkey fit and happy, you see. If it had been a ground monkey, Yuan wouldn't need a tree. You can keep a ground monkey quite happy by letting him jump about the furniture, and creep under cupboards and beds, for that's what a ground monkey likes.'

Ma Joong nodded slowly. He knew from their years together in the 'green woods' that Chiao Tai had a way with animals. He loved to make them tame and to study all their habits.

106

'All right,' he said, 'let's climb the damned pagoda. From up there we should be able to see in what section of this quarter there grow trees. It isn't much of a lead, but it's better than nothing.'

They went up the stone stairs again. A novice took them across the central courtyard, then to the entrance of the nine-storeyed pagoda behind the main hall. Sweating and cursing the two friends climbed the steep, narrow staircase. Arrived on the platform of the ninth storey, however, they found that the hot haze hanging over the sea of roofs had thinned out a little, so that the entire quarter was spread out below them like a pictorial map. They saw only one patch of green, away behind the temple, where there were nothing but slums. Beyond it a lonely banner hung limply from a high stake. It indicated the local military post.

'We shall head for that green patch, brother,' Chiao Tai said. 'Look, the roofs around it form a square and they are higher than those of the other houses. I think it's one of those very old mansions, dating from the time when this quarter was still the center of the city. Now a dozen or so poor families have found shelter in most of them.'

'Good. That's the kind of place Yuan would stay in. Let's try to work out how we get there.' Ma Joong leaned over the balustrade and peered at the maze of narrow streets and alleys deep down below. 'Yes, we must first make for that small square behind the temple, you see. Then take the winding road down there, and afterwards the straight alley to the left. If we follow that, we can't go far wrong.'

They began the long journey down, in a cheerful mood.

After half an hour of tramping up and down dirty streets, however, their spirits had sunk again. The farther they penetrated into the back streets, the poorer the houses became, and they met no one who they could ask for the way. At last they found, on a corner, an old hag, clad in rags. She was searching the smelly gutter for eatable offal. She had not seen any traveling puppeteers or acrobats about, but she told them that three streets ahead there stood indeed a large old house. 'It's a big affair,' she added, 'and squatters live in the back. There are no trees, though. The front yard is in a bad state; we put our dead there, till the scavengers come to collect them.' She pushed an untidy grey strand away from her sweating face and added: 'We are lucky, many scavengers gather here. They are good men, they can call up the souls of the dead, and they have amulets that protect you against all sickness.'

Chiao Tai thanked her, and they walked on. In the next street they met a group of about a dozen scavengers. Among them was a spare man, clad in a long robe of costly brocade and wearing a high cap of black gauze.

'Hey there, Doctor!' Ma Joong called out. 'What are you doing here?'

Doctor Lew said something to the tall hooded man by his side. Then he stepped up to the two friends and replied politely:

'I just went to see two young women, colonel, in the large old house over there. Couldn't do a thing, unfortunately. They had got the sickness, and died before my eyes.'

Ma Joong went pale. A sick feeling contracted his stomach.

'The two daughters of Yuan, you mean?' he asked.

'Yuan? Were they called Yuan?' Lew asked the tall hooded man. The other shrugged his shoulders, covered by the long black cloak.

'Show us the place, Doctor,' Chiao Tai ordered. 'I didn't know you looked so well after the poor.'

'I take my profession seriously,' the doctor said coldly. 'Follow me, if you insist on verifying my statement.'

They went on, the group of scavengers on their heels. After a while the tall hooded man came to walk by Chiao Tai's side. He said, his words muffled by the hood:

'I know you, Mister Colonel. You are the one who had four of us beheaded. In the square.'

'I'll have your head chopped off too,' Chiao Tai told

him. 'For an even smaller offense! Watch your step, my friend.'

The other fell behind. Chiao Tai heard him whisper to the other scavengers.

In the next street a dozen more hooded men joined them. They began to talk busily amongst each other in their muffled voices. Ma Joong looked around at them. Through the slits of the hoods their eyes fixed him with a malevolent glitter. He nudged his friend. Chiao Tai had his hand on the hilt of his sword. He too had noticed their threatening attitude.

'Here we are,' Doctor Lew spoke. He had halted in front of a dilapidated gate. The weather-beaten bricks showed through the burst plaster, but the door studded with nails seemed quite new. Lew pointed at the wooden crossbar. Two scavengers lifted it from its hinges and pushed the door open. The doctor went inside, followed by Ma Joong and Chiao Tai. The scavengers stayed outside, the narrow street was crammed by black hoods.

Ma Joong stepped up to the two still figures lying on a heap of refuse, at the entrance of the high, semi-dark vestibule. He heaved a deep sigh of relief. The dead women were completely unknown to him.

'The air is polluted here,' Chiao Tai told the doctor gruffly. 'The squatters must evacuate this compound.'

'You go and tell them, colonel! I'll say good-bye here. I also have my duties.'

'Not nice to have met you,' Ma Joong said sourly.

'You'd better be careful, Colonel,' Dr Lew told him venomously. 'You might need me, one of these days.'

'When we get sick,' Chiao Tai put in cheerfully, 'we'll call our coroner. He'll be overjoyed at having a squint at a live body, for a change!'

Doctor Lew turned around and went outside without another word.

The two friends walked down the long, narrow corridor. A little farther along the roof had caved in, leaving a large gap high above them through which they could see the sultry sky. The corridor had no windows, and the walls, though covered with mold, looked very solid. At the end was another door. Chiao Tai tried to push it open, but it would not budge. He put his ear to the wood. On the other side was the murmur of many voices. Suddenly there came a coarse voice from above:

'You are caught, dirty dogs!'

A hooded head was peering down at them through the gap in the roof. There was a swishing sound. An arrow missed Ma Joong's head by the fraction of an inch.

'Back to the gate!' Chiao Tai hissed.

They ran down the corridor as fast as they could. Ma Joong stepped over the two dead women and pulled at the door. It didn't move.

'They got us!' Chiao Tai whispered. 'The bastards have bows, and they can pick us off through the gap as if we were sitting ducks. Let's break the other door down, and fight our way through the crowd at the back.'

'Heaven knows what weapons they carry under those damned cloaks,' Ma Joong said hurriedly. 'And it's forty to two. That calls for strategy rather than force, brother. Help me to take off my coat of mail, quick!' He whispered a few instructions into Chiao Tai's ear, then shouted through the door: 'What do you think you are doing, bastards? Our soldiers will make mince-meat out of you!'

The scavengers outside jeered.

'We'll deliver the two of you neatly rolled up in canvas,' someone shouted. 'Nobody'll know, and no-body'll care!'

'Let's talk this over!' Ma Joong called back. He was helping Chiao Tai to put his own jacket of mail on one of the dead women. After Chiao Tai had put Ma Joong's helmet on her head, Ma Joong lifted her up, his hands under her arms. Chiao Tai stuck the point of his sword into the nape of her neck, just under the backflap of the helmet. 'Sorry, old girl,' he muttered. Then he walked up to the gap, holding the limp body up in front of him on his sword, both hands on the hilt. Ma Joong, clad only in his leather trousers and

110

MA JOONG AND CHIAO TAI VIEW TWO BODIES

an under-shirt, quickly inspected the bolt on the door. It was still in working order. When he looked around he saw two arrows hit the dead woman. Chiao Tai let her sink to the floor, then stepped forward and bent over her, keeping his face well down. An arrow struck his back, a second glanced off his helmet. He screamed, and let himself fall on top of the prostrate woman, then lay quite still.

'Got them both!' a voice shouted high above, on the roof.

Ma Joong who had pressed his back against the wall beside the door, now heard the sound of the crossbar being removed. The door opened, and a hooded man stepped inside. Ma Joong clasped his left arm round his head from behind and stuck his sword deep into his right flank. In practically the same moment he kicked the door shut. Letting the writhing body drop to the floor, he shot the bolt.

'What's wrong?' a voice sounded from outside.

Ma Joong had draped the black cloak of his victim around his shoulders and stuck the dagger the man had been carrying in his own belt. Putting the hood over his head he ran over to Chiao Tai who was lying motionless over the dead woman.

'Give me a hand!' he shouted up.

Two hooded heads appeared in the gap above him. A light bamboo ladder was lowered and Ma Joong quickly climbed up. The hooded men, both carrying a bow and arrows, were precariously perched on the narrow ridge of the roof. Ma Joong saw to his satisfaction that the ridge ran straight to the roof's rear.

'What's——' the tallest black man began.

Ma Joong gave him a vigorous push that sent him tumbling head over heels through the gap. He opened his cloak and buried the dagger he had taken from the man down in the corridor into the stomach of the other scavenger with all the force he could summon. He let go of the hilt, and threw him down into the corridor too. Gathering the cloak closely around him, he walked gingerly along the ridge to the small flat roof that marked the back entrance of the corridor. Looking

112

down at the two dozen hooded men that were crowding the small garden below, he shouted:

'Run for it! The soldiers are at the main gate!'

The men hesitated only a moment. When they heard the loud pounding on the iron-bound front gate, they scurried to the garden door.

Ma Joong walked back along the ridge as quickly as he dared. Surefooted as he was, he sighed with relief when he had safely reached the roof of the gatehouse.

'The soldiers are at the back gate!' he called out. 'Can't see anyone in the next street yet. If we hurry we can make it!'

A confused murmur of exclamations and curses came up to him. He quickly surveyed the black crowd. Doctor Lew was not among them.

He went to the gap and let himself slide down the bamboo ladder. Chiao Tai had already taken Ma Joong's jacket of mail off the dead woman, and wrapped it up in his neckcloth, together with the helmet. Now he was donning the black cloak of the tall scavenger Ma Joong had thrown down into the corridor first. The man's head was lying at an unnatural angle.

'Put the hood over your head and come along!' Ma Joong told his friend.

They climbed up the ladder, and surveyed the neighborhood. All the black men had melted away.

Following the ridge to the rear end of the corridor, they jumped into the garden. The gate proved to give access to a narrow alley.

'On to the military post!' Ma Joong gasped.

In the next street they suddenly met four scavengers.

'What side are the soldiers, brothers?' Chiao Tai asked.

'Everywhere! Run!' The four scavengers pushed them aside and scurried into a side street.

It took them quite some time before they had located the military post. They met only one ordinary citizen on the way. He quickly stood aside when he saw the two tall hooded figures approach.

They discarded their cloaks and hoods only when they were in the yard of the small inn where the guardsmen had established their headquarters. Chiao Tai and Ma Joong stripped naked and squatted on the stone floor. While two soldiers were sluicing them with cold water, two others fumigated their clothes and armor over the brazier with aromatic herbs they kept burning in the yard's corner.

Chiao Tai learned to his satisfaction from the lieutenant in charge that a horse was standing ready. That was part of the alarm system he and Ma Joong had devised: during daytime every post should have always a horse ready for carrying a message, and at night a few signal rockets that exploded into many colored lights. He ordered the lieutenant to dispatch a soldier on horseback to all the other posts in the vicinity, collect a hundred men and round up the scavengers in the quarter. 'Those who carry arms you arrest,' he added, 'and everyone who tries to put up resistance you cut down on the spot. Escort the lot to Military Police Headquarters.'

He winced as Ma Joong pasted an oil plaster on the wound in his back. The iron rings of the coat of mail had of course prevented the arrow from entering his body, but they had penetrated deep into the flesh.

'Lucky it was only an ordinary wooden arrow,' Ma Joong remarked. 'If it had been one of those new-type iron-shafted ones, its sheer force would've pushed in your carcass. Told Supply a hundred times that now that those new crossbows are used the coats of mail should have iron breast and back-plates. But they say you can't sacrifice mobility to safety, the stubborn bastards!'

All dressed up again, they ate a quick noonmeal with the lieutenant. Then they left the inn, and went back into the slums. Apparently the word had gotten around that there had been trouble. Here and there people had opened their windows, and were anxiously looking up and down the sordid street. By dint of much asking, they finally found their way to a large house in a narrow but fairly clean alley. The rickety front door was standing ajar.

The front hall was completely bare, and the plaster

hung down in large patches. But the floor had been swept clean of rubbish and dust. They surveyed the door openings of the small rooms on the left and right. The doors had apparently been taken down long ago to serve as firewood.

'No one about!' Chiao Tai muttered.

'Hush!' Ma Joong had raised his hand. In the rear of the compound someone was playing a flute.

They crossed the hall and threw the double doors at the end wide open. They gave access to a spacious but ill-kept garden. Peach and orange trees stood among the tall grass. An open corridor ran all along on the right and left, leading to a higher building in the back. This was indeed the square compound they had seen from the top of the pagoda. Now they could hear the flute better. It was played by an expert, a lively tune with a marked rhythm and an attractive lilt.

'Found them!' Chiao Tai said. He pointed up at the small brown monkey that was hanging by its tail from a branch overhead, keenly observing them with its round brown eyes. Chiao Tai made a purring sound, trying to coax it down. Ma Joong had run straight to the corridor on the left. The red lacquer was peeling off the low balustrades. Evidently the place had stood empty for a long time.

When Chiao Tai had overtaken him, he said dryly:

'I hope that wench of yours is at home. I am prepared to keep her father and sister busy, so that you can cuddle her in a corner. You deserve it. For once!'

Ma Joong grinned broadly. Coming from his taciturn blood brother, this was high praise indeed.

Arrived at the high building, they halted in their steps. Through the arched door opening a charming scene met their eyes. Yuan was playing a long flute, on a tabouret in the center of a spacious, high-ceilinged hall, empty but for a rustic wooden bench and a bamboo tea table in the corner. Coral, dressed in a long, flowing robe, was dancing on the tips of her diminutive embroidered shoes, gracefully waving her long sleeves. In the wall behind her was a moon door that gave onto an attractive miniature garden, where slender bamboos

CORAL'S DANCE

grew among a few quaintly shaped rocks. After the brutal violence of the encounter they had behind them, this peaceful scene seemed out of another world. They watched it, spellbound.

Finally Ma Joong stepped inside and cleared his throat. Yuan took the flute from his lips. He looked his two visitors up and down with raised eyebrows. Then he rose and came to meet them. Making a light bow, he asked in his deep voice:

'What gives us the honor of this unexpected visit?'

'Is your daughter Bluewhite here?' Ma Joong asked quickly.

Yuan bestowed a thoughtful glance on him.

'No,' he replied, 'she went out half an hour ago. Take a seat.' He pointed at the bench and said over his shoulder to his daughter: 'Fetch the tea-basket from the side room, Coral.'

Ma Joong was at a loss how to phrase their message. He tugged at his moustache, decided that it would be rude to come to the point abruptly, and temporized by remarking casually:

'We met a bunch of scavengers who seemed out for trouble, you know. Did you hear something about an incident?'

'No. The fellows are becoming a real nuisance, though. They have organized a kind of brotherhood, and force people to buy their faked amulets, pretending that they will make the wearer invulnerable. They add a lot of nonsense about the plague being a sure sign that Heaven has withdrawn its mandate from the Emperor, and that a new era is about to begin.' He shrugged. 'What if it were? There'll always be the rulers and the ruled, and the ruled will always come off losers!'

'Amen,' said Chiao Tai. Seeing Ma Joong's embarrassed look, he decided to take the initiative himself and resumed: 'We have come here with a message from our boss, the Lord Chief Justice. He wants to see you at once, Mr Yuan. And also your daughter Coral.'

'He does, does he?' Yuan said slowly. Coral came back, a tea-basket in her hand. She carried the small tea table over to them and poured two cups. Ma Joong thought she was a sweet-looking girl; but she lacked the proud, clean-cut beauty of her sister.

'These two gentlemen want to escort us to the Governor's palace,' her father told her.

In a frightened gesture, she covered her mouth with her sleeve.

'Our boss just wants to ask you a few questions,' Ma Joong told them hurriedly.

'What about the monkey?' Coral asked her father.

'He won't run away,' Yuan reassured her. 'He hasn't explored the neighborhood yet, and he won't dare to leave this garden. Bluewhite will look after him when she comes back. Let's go!'

While they were walking down the corridor, Yuan made a sweeping gesture and said:

'You can see that this was quite a nice residence, formerly. But the owner moved uptown, many years ago. Some squatters settled down here, but they left because the house was haunted, they said.' He shrugged his narrow shoulders. 'Never met a ghost here myself yet. The hall is fine for Coral's dancing, and her sister practices sword fighting in the garden.'

When they were stepping out into the street, a military patrol passed by, armed to the teeth. The rounding up of the scavengers had begun.

XVI

Judge Dee was sitting at his desk, signing the papers Tao Gan was handing him one by one. Seeing Ma Joong and Chiao Tai enter, the judge laid down his writing-brush and said:

'Hoo let himself be arrested quietly, this morning. It's long past noon. Did you manage to find that puppeteer?'

'Yes sir,' Ma Joong replied. 'He and his daughter Coral are waiting outside, in the ante-room. Her sister had gone out, and since you said you didn't need her, we didn't wait for her to come back. On our way out there, sir, we discovered that there's trouble brewing among the scavengers in that quarter. The bastards are organizing a kind of semi-religious brotherhood, selling charms and spreading all kinds of seditious rumors.'

The judge hit his fist on the table.

'It only needed that!' he exclaimed angrily. 'Seditious religious sects!' He checked himself and resumed quietly: 'We must take adequate measures at once. In a time like this, those sects spread like wildfire. Open rebellion often starts that way.'

'We had something of a scuffle with them out there, sir,' Chiao Tai added. 'When we discovered that they were carrying concealed weapons, we went to the local military post, and told them to alarm the other posts in that neighborhood. They are rounding up the scoundrels now. Presently Brother Ma and I will go to Military Police Headquarters and question the prisoners.'

'Doctor Lew was there too, sir,' Ma Joong resumed. 'He seemed to be on quite good terms with those hoodlums. But he disappeared when the trouble started. So I don't know for sure whether he is hand in glove with them.'

'Verify that when you are interrogating the prisoners,' Judge Dee told him. 'Let me have your report as soon as you are through over there. Now, fetch Yuan and his daughter.'

On a sign from the judge Chiao Tai and Tao Gan pulled up two stools and sat down by the side of his desk.

'Mr Yuan and his daughter, sir,' Ma Joong announced.

Yuan knelt, and Coral followed his example.

'You may rise!' the judge told them. Yuan scrambled

119

up and stood there with an impassive face, his hands by his sides. He studied the judge with wary eyes. Coral hung her head, her slender hands played nervously with the ends of her silk sash. Judge Dee noticed that she wore a small piece of plaster on her right ear.

'Your name is Coral, isn't it?' he asked her.

She nodded silently.

'Usually twins are given similar names. Why didn't you follow this time-honored custom, Mr Yuan?'

'Originally my wife called them Sapphire and Coral, my lord. Thirteen years ago, however, a woman called Sapphire disappeared from a brothel in the old city under mysterious circumstances. Since I was afraid that the name would bring bad luck to my child, I changed hers into Bluewhite, which refers to the color of the stone.'

'I see.' The judge took the ear-pendant and the red stone from his drawer and laid them on the desk.

'How did you lose these?' he asked Coral.

She raised her head. When her eyes fell on the trinkets, her rosy cheeks suddenly turned chalk white.

'All right,' Judge Dee said curtly. 'You may wait in the ante-room. Take her there, Tao Gan.'

While his lieutenant was leading her outside, the judge looked Yuan over, slowly stroking his moustache. At last he asked:

'What was your relation with the bondmaid who was whipped to death by Yee six years ago?'

'She was my wife,' Yuan replied quietly.

'How did she become a bondmaid?'

'Because I couldn't pay Mr Hoo the money I owed him.'

Judge Dee raised his eyebrows.

'Hoo, you say?'

'Yes, my lord. Mr Hoo employed my late father as his steward. The salary was low, our family large. Bitter poverty made my father steal money from a goldsmith. Mr Hoo hushed it up and refunded the stolen money to its rightful owner. In return for this favor, my father agreed to pay him back double the amount, in monthly installments. My father died after

120

he had paid the first installment, so the debt devolved on me. Owing to the expenses of my father's burial, I could not pay on time, and Mr Hoo ruled that my wife would serve him as bondmaid, her wages being deducted from the debt. Hoo treated her well, on the whole. Once, however, Yee saw her when he visited Hoo, and he asked Hoo to transfer the bond to him. That is how my wife then became Yee's bondmaid.'

'Why didn't you protest?' the judge asked sharply. 'The transfer of bonds is illegal.'

'How could I have done that, sir?' Yuan asked, astonished. 'Mr Hoo was our master and our benefactor. Hadn't he saved my late father's reputation by making good the theft?'

'Why then didn't you denounce Yee after he had murdered your wife in that abominable manner?'

'I, a steward's son, denounce Marquis Yee, the lord of the "old world"?' Yuan scoffed. 'High up here in your palace, my lord, you know very little indeed about the kind of justice meted out by the minions of the law to us, the poor.'

'I try to keep myself informed,' the judge said dryly. 'Abuses are punished severely, but we cannot prosecute if the people don't denounce offenders. A gong hangs in the gatehouse of the High Court, and at the gate of every tribunal in the empire, and every citizen has the right to beat that gong to announce that he wants to report an injustice. That is not only his privilege, but also his civic duty. There is impartial justice in the empire, Mr Yuan. Has been for the last two thousand years, if you except periods of national crisis and upheaval.'

'Living as I do in the slums of the old city, that fact must have escaped my attention,' the puppeteer said dully.

'If you had gone to my predecessor, six years ago, you would have noticed it all right,' Judge Dee said unperturbed. 'Then there would have been no need to arrange an elaborate kind of marionette-play, involving a degrading experience for your young daughter, and exposing her to grave risks.'

121

As Yuan remained silent, the judge went on:

'Being a puppeteer, you imagined that human beings can be manipulated in the same way as your marionettes. You knew Hoo's violent temper and his crude sensual appetites, as well as Yee's perverted lusts. You thought that, through your daughter, you could stir up trouble between those two, and that Hoo would kill Yee, or Yee Hoo. In either case your wife would have been avenged, for the murderer would have been executed. For achieving that purpose you did not shrink from making your daughter, a sweet young girl, expose herself naked to two evil lechers, apart from the risk that one of them would simply violate her on the spot.'

'Coral did not mind taking risks, sir. She was very fond of her mother, and she would do anything to avenge her. She fully approved my plan, for it meant avenging her mother without me or she actually raising our hand against our former masters. And as regards dancing in the nude, that also is a fine art. It does not degrade the serious performer. Only the wrong kind of spectator.'

'Suppose one of those lechers had tried to overpower her up there in the gallery?'

'The keeper of the Tavern of the Five Blessings always went with her, my lord. He is my best friend, and he can play the drum very well.'

'I saw him!' Ma Joong exclaimed angrily. 'An undersized hunchback! And you entrusted him with . . .'

'That hunchback is the best knife-thrower in the city, Mr Ma,' Yuan interrupted him with quiet dignity. 'And a man without fear. Further, Yee was firmly convinced that Coral was a professional courtesan and the hunchback her tout. He bargained several times with him, as a matter of fact, about buying Coral. Yee thought she would be his to do what he liked with as soon as the price was agreed upon.'

'Did your other duaghter know about your scheme?' Judge Dee asked.

'Heaven forbid, sir!' Yuan exclaimed aghast. 'I had always told her that her mother met with an accident while working for Yee, that she fell into a deep well.

122

If Bluewhite had known the truth, she would have gone to Yee at once and strangled him with her own hands! She is a good straightforward girl, sir, but she has a violent temper and she is awfully strong-minded. If she has set her mind to do something, even I, her father, can't keep her back. Coral is quite different, she is a meek and docile girl, her main interest is in singing and dancing.' He shook his head resignedly, and went on: 'All went well until last night. Coral went there without telling me, and all alone. She . . .'

'I prefer to hear the rest from her own mouth,' the judge interrupted him. 'Bring her in again, Tao Gan!'

When she was standing before him again, Judge Dee said to her:

'Your father has just told me about the plan to avenge your mother, Miss Yuan. Now I want to hear from you exactly what happened last night.'

She gave the judge a timid look and began in a soft voice:

'Yesterday, at noon, I went to the market with my twin sister, my lord. We wanted to see if we could find some vegetables. All of a sudden, someone tugged at my sleeve from behind. It was Mr Yee. I was in a dead fright, but he smiled at me and said in a pleasant voice: "How are you, Coral? And this is your twin sister Bluewhite, isn't it? The famous girl-acrobat. I knew your father well, you know, when he was serving in the house of my good friend Hoo." I couldn't imagine how he could have discovered my identity, and I was at a loss what to say. I just dropped a low curtsy, and so did my sister. Then, after some desultory conversation, Yee said that he wanted to talk to me alone for a moment, about an old family affair. As soon as my sister had walked on to have a look at the stalls, Yee's manner changed. He called me awful names and said that one of his retainers had seen me when going to his place. The man had recognized me as Yuan's daughter, and informed Yee. "Your father always was a tricky bastard," he hissed. Then he went on to tell me that he would inform Mr Hoo, and that they would kidnap my father and torture him to death. I begged him to forgive

123

us. At last he said: "All right. I promise that I shall leave your father in peace. On condition that you dance once more for me. Come tonight, and alone, mind you".'

A fiery blush had colored her cheeks. Looking up at the judge, she said meekly:

'I knew full well that Yee's order meant more than dancing, sir. But I would gladly have surrendered to him, for it meant my father's life. So I promised I would come. I told my sister a fancy story. In the evening I said to my father that I was going out to meet a girl friend. I arrived in the Yee mansion at the appointed time. I had taken my guitar with me, because I hoped I would be able to gain time by playing some music for him. He let me inside himself. He was in a pleasant mood again, and chatted with me about all kinds of trifles when he was taking me up to the dressing-room of the gallery. I proposed to play and sing for him first, but he would have none of that. He said with a smile that I needn't be afraid, he just wanted to see me dance for the last time, that was all.

'I undressed and stepped out into the gallery. Yee was sitting at the table, in his armchair. I saw that he had moved the couch from the wall to the center of the partico. Evidently he intended to tease Hoo again by making me dance on that couch, so that Hoo could see me from his balcony. And indeed Yee pointed at the couch.

'I stepped onto it, but didn't know how to begin, for there was no drum to dance to. Yee tasted from the ginger on the table, he let me stand there for a long time, horribly embarrassed. Suddenly he said with a smile: "Come here and have some ginger too. It's quite good."

'As soon as I had come up to the table he suddenly jumped up. He grabbed me by my hair with his left hand, so roughly that one of my ear-pendants was torn off. Taking the whip he had hidden behind him in the chair, he called me the vilest words from the gutter, shouting that he would kill me in exactly the same manner as he had killed my mother, and on the self-

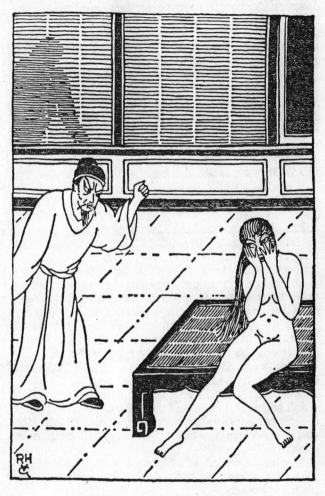

A CRUEL TYRANT AND HIS VICTIM

same couch. He let go of my hair, and lashed me with the whip across my breast. I stumbled back and sank down on the couch, covering my face with my hands, in abject fear. Suddenly Yee's raving broke off. Looking through my fingers I saw that Yee had half turned to the windows of the portico. A huge, dark shadow had appeared on the bamboo curtain.

'I quickly got up. Clutching my breast I slipped into the dressing-room. I grabbed my clothes and my guitar and ran downstairs as fast as I could. In the passage downstairs I dressed somehow or other, then ran across the courtyard. No one was there. I went outside through the narrow door in the gate, pulling it shut behind me.'

She heaved a deep sigh. Ma Joong offered her a cup of tea. But she shook her head and resumed:

'I aimlessly walked through the empty streets, trying to think out what had happened. Evidently Mr Hoo had been spying on Yee. When he saw me standing naked on the couch, his violent temper got the better of him. He must have jumped into the canal and climbed up on the balcony. Then, however, Yee must have told him who I really was, and that would have made them patch up their quarrel, the two men sitting down together to devise a horrible scheme for ruining us. I became panicky again, and tried to keep up my spirits by singing a little song. Then those two awful scavengers tried to assault me, and then that doctor . . . It was the most wretched night I ever had.'

Tears were glittering in her eyes. She wiped them off impatiently and went on:

'Fortunately my sister was not at home. My father didn't scold me, but he said that we would have to leave the city at once, to escape the vengeance of Mr Hoo and Yee. When we heard that Yee had been murdered . . .'

Her voice trailed off. She cast a shy look at the judge. He was leaning back in his chair, slowly caressing his side-whiskers.

'Thank you, Miss Yuan,' he spoke. 'It was indeed a terrible experience. However, you are a plucky girl, and you are very young. The young easily forget, a

privilege not shared by older persons, unfortunately.'
Turning to the puppeteer, he asked in a gentle voice:
'Why did you include that hideous scene of your wife's
murder in your peepshow?'

'To keep my hatred alive, my lord,' Yuan replied at
once. Then he looked away. The lines of his mobile
actor's face suddenly deepened. He resumed, awk-
wardly groping for words: 'I have some . . . some
doubts, at times. About things, in general. I think of
the milieu Yee was reared in, the "old world", with all
its antiquated ideas of absolute power, all its frustra-
tion. . . .' He looked at the judge and said apologeti-
cally: 'It's my puppets that give me those strange ideas,
I fear. When I met Mr Ma in the tavern, I had been
brooding again. And suddenly I felt that I had to look
again at . . . at that incident, had to talk about it.' He
shook his head. His voice was firm again when he concluded: 'Well, my scheme was indeed successful, after
all. Hoo and Yee must have got into a violent quarrel.
Hoo murdered Yee, and you have arrested him already,
I hear. I fully understand that I shall have to accept
the consequences of my actions, my lord.'

Judge Dee studied his drawn face for a while. Suddenly he asked Coral:

'Did Yee pay you for your performances, Miss
Yuan?'

'No sir. He wanted to several times. But Hunchback
Wang always told him that it would be included in the
final settlement.'

'In that case,' the judge said, 'there is no charge
against you, Mr Yuan, nor against your daughter. It
was wrong of you to try to take justice in your own
hands, but it would be most difficult to construct a case
against you on that ground. Moreover, who shall say
whether Yee and Hoo did not have other bones to pick
between the two of them, apart from their jealousy
over your daughter? As for her, there is no rule for-
bidding a girl to dance gratis, even in the nude. Here,
take these trinkets, Miss Yuan. The red coral goes well
with your name!'

Yuan wanted to speak, but the judge raised his hand.

'Yee was a despicable relic of an abominable age,' Judge Dee said gravely. 'And yet, Mr Yuan, the impartial justice I just spoke of requires that his murderer, although he freed the world of a cruel monster, shall be beheaded, unless he can prove it to have been manslaughter. For if people were allowed to take justice in their own hands, the rule of law would cease, and everybody would be at his neighbor's mercy. I have arrested Hoo because he tried to assault your daughter Bluewhite——'

'Mr Hoo assaulted Bluewhite?' Yuan exclaimed. 'When——'

'You had better ask her that yourself,' Judge Dee said curtly.

'The wench never tells me anything!' the puppeteer said angrily.

'Anyway,' the judge went on, 'attempted rape is a capital charge, so Hoo's head shall fall on the scaffold. Tell your daughter that I said that. It will set her mind at rest. You may go.'

Yuan and his daughter fell on their knees and began to thank the judge. But he told them to rise and said:

'If you want to do me a favor, Mr Yuan, then make it known in the "old world" that there is justice for high and low, rich and poor. And that even in a time like the present, when hundreds die from the plague every day, the death of every single person who dies by violence shall be duly investigated and avenged. Goodbye!'

Ma Joong saw the puppeteer and his daughter out. He came back and exclaimed with a beaming smile:

'How ever did you discover what happened, sir?'

Judge Dee sat back in his chair.

'Your account of the meeting in the tavern,' he replied, 'told me that Yuan was emotionally involved in the bondmaid's killing. So deeply involved that he simply *had* to show that scene and speak about its horrors—even to a complete stranger like you. If he had known that you were one of my lieutenants, it would have been different. In that case I would have assumed that the crime had nothing to do with him, but that, having heard about it, he wanted to get Yee punished for his iniquities, and that he therefore made the picture for his peepshow, hoping for an opportunity to bring the crime in this manner to the knowledge of an official and thus arouse his interest in this old case. Such a roundabout method would have been just what one would expect from an ordinary man of the people.

'Second, when I discovered that Yee's maid Cassia had caught Hoo's fancy once, I realized that her testimony had been calculated to lead us astray by a clever mixture of truth and falsehood. After she had found Yee's body, she had evidently had a look around the gallery for possible clues to the murderer. She understood that he must have been a strong man, and when she saw the wet marks on the windowsill, she suspected at once that Hoo had done it, having entered the gallery by the balcony. Therefore she wiped the windowsill clean. In her hurry she overlooked the bloodstained piece of cloth lying behind the pillar. When she was telling her son about the murder, she remembered the dancing girl and the tout the boy had seen, and she decided to lead suspicion away from Hoo by suggesting that the tout was the murderer. She mentioned that possibility to her son, but he said that the tout was a small man. She persuaded the youngster that the darkness had deceived him, and that the tout was really a big bully, like most men of that profession: he was to describe the man as such when the constables questioned him. But the boy was not quite convinced that the shadows had indeed played him a trick, and he was also afraid to cause trouble to the girl he admired. Hence his nervousness when I questioned him about the girl and her companion. That Hoo described the tout as an elderly, high-shouldered man ought to have set me thinking at once.

'Thereafter, however, I combined a number of seemingly unrelated and even contradictory facts, and suddenly everything fell into place. Our reptilian friend of the Special Service convinced me that Porphyry was a faked courtesan, who had evidently acted that part expressly to sow discord between Hoo and Yee. Yuan

had a daughter named Coral who was a good singer—
I heard her myself in the street below here—and Yee's
doorman had been much impressed by Porphyry's
sweet voice. Finally, porphyry and coral are similar
stones. When adopting a faked name, people have a
tendency to select one that resembles the real name:
an intuitive, mystic fear of losing one's identity by
using a wholly different name, I assume. Therefore I
concluded that the murdered bondmaid must have
been a near relative of Yuan, and that he, being a
puppeteer, had wanted to stage a plot of private vengeance, using Coral as the main actress. The emergency
was the ideal time for executing the scheme, for Yee
had sent nearly all his servants away, and the prosti-
tutes from the brothels refused to come. Yuan's mistake
was that he wanted to take over the responsibility of
the Playwright.' The judge smiled wanly and added: 'I
should be the last to blame him for that, though!
Heaven knows that I make that mistake too, on occasion! Well, let's have a cup of tea. Then I must change,
for it's getting time to go to the Mei residence for the
funeral service.'

'With your permission, sir,' Ma Joong said, 'I would
like to go with Brother Chiao to the military police
now. To inquire how the rounding up of the scavengers
went.'

'By all means. Call on the municipal chancery first,
though. They must order our friend Mr Fang to coun-
termand his instructions for the apprehension of "Porphyry" and her companion. Otherwise Mr Yuan and
Coral will be waylaid by all kinds of thugs and plug-
uglies from the licensed quarters, eager to earn the
reward! Tao Gan, you will accompany me to the Mei
mansion.'

XVII

'I received the impression,' Tao Gan said in his cautious manner, 'that Mrs Mei made an excellent hostess. A dignified widow, I must say. Ex-courtesan or not.'

Judge Dee did not reply. Dusk had fallen. They were sitting at the balustrade of the western terrace of the Mei residence. From this platform, raised two feet above the level of the garden, they had a magnificent view of the flowering trees planted along the meandering footpaths that criss-crossed the garden right up to the moss-covered wall in the rear. Beyond the garden wall loomed the roofs and turrets of the old city, black silhouettes against the grey, threatening sky.

From the reception hall behind them came the monotonous chant of the Buddhist monks. Seated in front of the high bier where Mei was lying in state, they recited the service of the dead, punctuating their chant with sharp raps on their skull-shaped wooden hand-gongs. The dead man's cousin had received the few mourners that had been able to come, mostly representatives of the charitable institutions that Mei had endowed, and a sprinkling of notables. Mrs Mei had stood modestly in the background, very tall and slender in her white mourning robe. From the high rafters overhead hung a profusion of white banners, proclaiming in large letters the many virtues of the deceased. Judge Dee had paid his last respect to the dead man by adding a pinch of powdered incense to the large bronze burner that stood on the altar table in front of the bier. Soon after that, however, he had taken Tao Gan outside to the garden terrace, for the pungent smell of the strong Indian

131

incense had given him a dull headache. The air in the garden was just as close as inside, but the quiet, deserted terrace was a pleasant change after the crowded hall.

'Strange,' Judge Dee spoke up suddenly. 'I had tea with Mei here on this terrace only three weeks ago. He told me that he had personally supervised the lay-out of this garden. He was a man of many talents. How well those clusters of bamboo are placed, harmonizing with the mossy stones in the rear!' He looked up at the almond trees, laden with white blossoms that spread a subtle fragrance, and pursued: 'It seems so incongruous, Tao Gan. This profusion of fresh flowers in this city of the dead.' He heaved a sigh, and said smoothing his long beard, 'You spoke of Mrs Mei, just now. Yes, she is a remarkable woman. I wonder what her plans are. I advised her to close down this mansion, and to move to their mountain villa.'

'I think she has decided to move to another city, sir. The cousin has brought a few maidservants along. They are now packing Mrs Mei's personal belongings.'

'Well, Mr Mei possessed a house in nearly every major city, so his widow can pick and choose.' He paused to reflect. After a while he said: 'I had been planning to have a look at the scene of Merchant Mei's accident, some time. Since we are here, we might as well do it now. Especially since Mrs Mei is planning to leave, as you just told me. Most of the mourners will have gone by now, and . . .' Suddenly he broke off and laid his hand on Tao Gan's arm. 'Look!' he said in a tense voice.

He pointed at a few white almond blossoms that came fluttering down from the branches overhead. Slowly they settled on the marble balustrade of the terrace. The judge rose, and lifted his hand.

'There does indeed seem to be a little movement in the air!'

Narrowing his eyes Tao Gan peered up at the sky.

'Yes, that big dark cloud there does seem to have shifted a bit, sir!'

'Heaven grant that this means a change of weather!'

132

the judge said fervently. 'Come along, let's go and find the housemaster.'

They went inside. In the front courtyard a few guests were still standing about in small groups, talking in undertones. The judge went straight to the housemaster, who was hovering near the gate. He told him to take them to the main hall of the east wing.

The old man led them through a long corridor to a hall of impressive dimensions. In the center a monumental marble staircase descended from the floor above, where there was a gallery lined by a red-lacquered balustrade, consisting of lattice-work of an intricate design. Still higher there was a kind of dome, crossed by two heavy rafters. From these hung an enormous red lampion that filled the entire hall with an agreeable diffuse light. The staircase was built in antique style, quite steep, and with marble bannisters only two feet high. At regular intervals the bannisters had newels, their tops carved into the shape of a lotus bud. The white-plastered wall on either side of the staircase was decorated by large silk hangings, embroidered with mythical representations. On the other side was a round door opening, a so-called moon door, its panels of lattice work pasted over with thin white silk. Beside the moon door stood a high wall table of carved ebony, carrying a flower vase.

The housemaster pointed at the left newel, at the bottom of the stairs.

'The master was found here, my lord,' he said in a hushed voice.

The judge nodded and looked up at the flight of white stairs.

'Very steep indeed,' he remarked. 'Mr Mei's library is somewhere upstairs, I suppose?'

'Indeed, my lord. It is the largest room of those lining the gallery, right opposite the head of the stairs. The other rooms up there are smaller, and used mainly for storage.'

Craning his neck the judge looked with interest at the colossal red lampion. On either side was written

133

one large character, the one reading 'Good Luck', the other 'Prosperity'.

'How do you manage to light that lampion?' he asked curiously.

'Oh, that's quite simple, my lord! Every evening at seven o'clock I go up to the gallery, and haul the lampion towards me with a long, hooked stick. I remove the stumps of the burned-down candles, and replace them with new ones. I use thick temple candles, which last till about midnight.'

Tao Gan had been feeling with his thin fingers the pointed top of the newel at the foot of the stairs. 'Even if Mr Mei's head had not struck this newel,' he remarked, 'the fall alone would have sufficed to kill him. Hitting his head on the edge of one of the steps, or on the marble floor down here would have been fatal, from that height.'

The judge nodded. He glanced at the three characters inscribed on the wooden board over the moon door. They read 'Abode of Elegant Leisure'. 'Excellent calligraphy,' he remarked.

'They were written by my late husband,' a soft voice spoke up. It was Mrs Mei. Doctor Lew stood beside her. He made a low bow.

'The staircase is very steep indeed, madam,' Judge Dee said. 'And the bannisters are too low to take hold of, should one miss one's step.'

'I do not think, my lord, that higher bannisters would have saved Mr Mei,' Doctor Lew observed. 'He must have had a stroke when about to descend. Most probably he was already dead when his head hit the newel.'

The judge turned to Mrs Mei.

'Could we perhaps see your late husband's library, madam? I would like very much to see the place where my valued friend used to read and write.'

It was a courteous request. But Tao Gan did not fail to notice the hard glint in Judge Dee's eyes. He wondered what the judge had just heard or seen that had put him suddenly on the alert.

'Certainly, sir!' Mrs Mei said. She gave a sign to the housemaster, who preceded them upstairs. 'Be careful, my lord!' he warned the judge when he stepped onto the gallery. 'There's still some wax on the floor, from the candle my master let drop there.' He cast a timid glance at Mrs Mei, who was coming up behind the judge, and added: 'I had meant to clean up here myself, but with my illness . . .'

Shaking his head he pushed the double door open and ushered the judge and Tao Gan into a large room, dimly lit by the red lampion in the hall. Judge Dee saw vaguely that the walls on the left and right were covered from floor to ceiling by solid antique bookcases of polished ebony. Against the back wall stood a broad couch of the same material, on top of it a thick reed mat and a white silk pillow. On the wall above the couch hung a large painting of the Abode of the Immortals, darkened by age.

Judge Dee went to the desk of carved ebony that stood in the center of the thick-piled, dark-blue carpet and sat down in the large armchair behind it, facing the door. On his left stood a high floor-lamp, with a pear-shaped shade of white silk. He took up the book that was lying open on the desk, but found that the light coming through the door was insufficient to read by. 'Light the floor-lamp for me,' he told the house-master.

While the old man lit the lamp with his tinderbox, the judge leafed the book through. Now he put it down and said to Mrs Mei, who had remained standing by the door, together with Doctor Lew:

'Here is another proof of your husband's devotion to public welfare, madam. This book, the last he read before his demise, is a medical treatise on how to combat epidemic diseases. Truly a great man!'

He bent over the desk, and began to examine all the writing implements and small ornaments with meticulous care. He took up the ink-slab, a small oval piece of stone of about half an inch thick, and admired the delicate carving of the tiny plumblossoms that decorated the rim. Passing his finger over the perfectly clean surface of the stone, he made an appreciative remark on its fine quality. Then he looked at the white, new

135

writing-brush, the small paperweight of green jade, and the water container of white porcelain. He did all this in a casual manner. But Tao Gan realized that the judge was looking for something. Peering over his shoulder, his hands behind his back, the thin man followed every movement. But try as he might, he could not guess what exactly the judge was trying to find.

At last Judge Dee got up. He cast a last, sweeping glance at the room and said with satisfaction:

'Everything here breathes a spirit of antique elegance.' Tao Gan had come to know his chief very well. He concluded from his mien that he had not found what he had expected to discover in the library.

They went down the marble staircase. When they were standing in the hall again, Mrs Mei said:

'My cousin is waiting in the front hall, my lord. Tea and refreshments are served there. I hope your lordship will allow me to retire now, I . . .'

The judge did not seem to have heard her. Pointing at the moon door, he asked the housemaster:

'What is the room over there used for?'

'It's our best guest-room, sir. It's rarely used, only for the master's old friends, as a matter of fact. It's not large, but it offers complete privacy. For it has a door that gives access to the side garden, connected with the street outside by a small gate. Thus the guests can come and go as they like.'

'Show me that room,' the judge said curtly.

'It'll be very untidy, my lord!' Mrs Mei protested. 'No one has used it these last weeks, and the maids . . .'

Judge Dee had already gone to the moon door and pushed its lattice door open. He remained standing just beyond the threshold, his arms folded in his wide sleeves. He took in the enormous bedstead on the left, closed by blue satin curtains that hung down to the white marble floor from the elaborately carved ebony canopy, high up under the raftered ceiling. The bedstead was flanked by a clothes-rack and a washing-stand with a brass basin. When his eye fell on the large dressing-table against the wall opposite, beside a narrow door, he walked straight over to it, followed on his heels by Tao Gan.

The judge cast a cursory glance at the round mirror of polished silver on its black lacquered stand, but the row of small porcelain boxes containing cosmetics seemed to arouse his interest. He opened every one of them, inspecting the powder and different kinds of rouge inside. He seemed completely oblivious of Mrs Mei and Doctor Lew, who were standing by the bedstead, watching Judge Dee with blank faces. The judge now directed his attention to the set for painting eyebrows beside the mirror: a large, square ink-slab of more than two inches thick and five inches square, a thin writing-brush, the cake of ink on its small wooden stand, and the silver water container for moistening the ink-slab prior to rubbing the ink. The surface of the slab was caked with dried ink, and the tip of the brush was black.

He turned around, walked over to the bedstead and parted the blue curtains. A crumpled white silk cover was lying across the bedmat, a red brocade pillow was pushed into a corner. There was a smell of stale cosmetics.

Mrs Mei beckoned the housemaster, who had remained outside.

'Tell the maids to have this room cleaned and aired at once!' she told him in a vexed voice.

The housemaster came hurriedly inside.

'Certainly, madam! Is there something wrong, my lord?' He stared, astonished, at the judge. About to close the bed-curtains again, he had all of a sudden checked himself. He was standing stock-still, his eyes on the floor. Now he stooped, lifted the left curtain's seam, and scrutinized the marble flag just underneath, directly beside the heavy front leg of the bedstead, carved in the shape of a huge lion's paw. Righting himself, he curtly told Tao Gan:

'Have a look at those grey stains on the marble!'

Tao Gan squatted. He wetted the tip of his forefinger and rubbed the stains. He stood up and said:

'It's ink, sir. Old stains. They have been wiped off,

JUDGE DEE IN THE GUEST ROOM OF THE MEI MANSION

but the ink had soaked into the marble. They ought to be scrubbed with sand, then they'll disappear completely.'

Judge Dee was still holding the seam of the curtain in his hand. Now he brought it close to his eyes and examined the smooth satin. Then he turned it over. Nodding slowly he showed Tao Gan a large, dark-brown stain, on the reverse of the seam.

He let the curtain drop, and looked fixedly at Mrs Mei.

'Your husband died here in this room, madam, he said coldly. 'Murdered.'

Mrs Mei's face turned deadly pale. She quickly stepped back, to Doctor Lew, who was standing still as a graven image.

'Yes, he was murdered,' the judge repeated. 'He was struck down by a blow of that heavy square ink-slab on the dressing-table there. His crushed skull hit the floor right here by this leg of the bedstead. The marble was stained by his blood and by the ink that had been rubbed on the slab shortly before it was used as a murder weapon. Blood and ink were wiped up, but the traces of the ink remained. The seam of the curtain had swept the blood, and the red stain on its reverse remained unnoticed.' Turning to the doctor, he added: 'This, incidentally, explains the ink smudges on the dead man's cheek, Doctor.'

Mrs Mei remained silent; she was staring at the judge with wide, unbelieving eyes. Doctor Lew spoke up, nervously:

'I could think of at least a dozen other explanations for the facts you mention, sir! You are famous for your logical mind, my lord. Surely you wouldn't distress Mrs Mei with a foolhardy statement, based on such flimsy evidence?'

The judge gave him a scornful look.

'Of course I would not do that,' he said quietly. 'The clues found here are only secondary evidence. The main point is that you and Mrs Mei lied to me about the time of Mr Mei's death. You stated that Mrs Mei found her husband's body at the bottom of the stairs in the hall at about ten o'clock. That means that he fell down the staircase before that time. But why should he then have taken a burning candle with him, when he left his library to go downstairs? The hall and the gallery upstairs are lit fairly well by the large red lampion, and it burns till midnight.' As Mrs Mei and Dr Lew looked at him, dumbfounded, he crossed his arms and spoke: 'Mrs Mei and Doctor Lew, I arrest you two for the murder of Mr Mei Liang. Call the soldiers who carried our sedan chair, Tao Gan!'

XVIII

About half an hour before the night session of the tribunal, Tao Gan was helping Judge Dee to put on his ceremonial robe, in the ante-room of his private office. Handing the judge his winged cap, Tao Gan remarked:

'I never liked that doctor, sir.'

'Neither did I,' the judge replied dryly. He carefully adjusted the cap in front of the special mirror, mounted on the black lacquered box in which the cap was kept.

'You went to Mei's library to look for a possible murder weapon, didn't you, sir?'

Judge Dee turned around.

'I went there in the first place to verify whether Mei had been writing something just before his death. I was thinking of the black smudges on his cheek, you see. As you yourself pointed out to me, the ink might have spattered accidentally onto his face while he was preparing it by rubbing the ink-cake on the stone slab. I found that he had been reading, however, and that the ink-slab and writing brush on his desk were perfectly clean. I then knew that his head must have been bashed in by another ink-slab; a large and heavy one, that had been used shortly before the murder, and therefore was still wet with ink. I found the murder weapon in the guest-room downstairs.' He looked out through the window and said disconsolately: 'The weather isn't changing, after all.'

'When did you begin to suspect that Mei had been murdered, sir?' Tao Gan asked keenly.

The judge folded his arms.

'Until the housemaster had told me that the lampion in the hall burns till midnight, I had only a vague feeling that something was wrong. A real accident, Tao Gan, can rarely be reconstructed as completely as that which allegedly happened to Mr Mei, you see. Consider the candle dropped at the head of the stairs, the slipper halfway down, the blood on the top of the newel, and the dead man's head lying close to that newel! It was all too pat. It seemed as if someone had deliberately charted the way it happened, so to speak, step by step. Further, the fact that Mrs Mei was a former courtesan and that her husband was twice her age, brought to mind, of course, the all too familiar trio: old husband, young wife, secret lover. That I gave Mrs Mei the benefit of the doubt was because of my high opinion of Mr Mei's staunch character and brilliant mind. I assumed that a man like him would never have chosen the wrong woman. Unfortunately I was quite wrong.'

'The guest-room downstairs was an ideal place for clandestine amorous meetings,' Tao Gan observed.

'That is why I insisted on seeing the room, as soon as the housemaster had told me that it had a back door that gave access to the garden and the street. I did indeed find there all the clues I needed. Mrs Mei had said herself that the room had not been occupied for weeks. Yet the dressing-table had been used quite recently, and by a woman. The covers of the porcelain powder boxes still bore the traces of fingertips, and the set for painting eyebrows had been recently used. And the bedstead had been slept in. The stain on the floor and on the curtain provided the final clues to what had actually happened. Old Mr Mei had evidently surprised

141

the lovers at midnight or thereafter, and one of them killed him by striking his head with the heavy ink-slab, the other acting as accomplice. Then they dragged his dead body to the hall and deposited it at the bottom of the staircase. All was dark there, hence their mistake about the candle Mei had allegedly been carrying.'

Judge Dee paused. Giving his lieutenant a shrewd look, he resumed:

'Trying to make a crime too perfect is a mistake of many murderers Tao Gan. They will try to lead investigators astray by adding superfluous details, not realizing that it's exactly those that arouse suspicion. In this case the candle, the slipper, and the blood on the newel were quite superfluous. As you pointed out very correctly when we were standing in the hall, Tao Gan, the fall from those steep stairs would have proved fatal to an old man like Mei anyway. Anybody who would find him at the foot of the stairs with a crushed skull, would have accepted it as death by accident. It was the superfluous clues that did for them.' He nodded pensively and continued: 'Doctor Lew made that mistake twice, as a matter of fact. The second time was when I talked with him alone in the Yee mansion, after Mrs Yee's suicide. I then asked Lew whether Mrs Mei was an ex-courtesan. Mr Fang had told me already that she had indeed been a courtesan, and I asked Lew only in order to make him talk about her, so as to find out more about their relationship. For I then had only a very vague feeling that there was something wrong with Mr Mei's accident. Lew could just have replied that he did not know anything about Mrs Mei's antecedents— which would have left me exactly where I was. When, however, he emphatically denied that she was an ex-courtesan, and told me a cock and bull story about her belonging to an old and distinguished family, and having married old Mei against her father's will, I understood that he knew everything about her real past. His telling me a perfectly superfluous string of lies suggested that he wanted to protect her against being suspected of the crime that comes to mind first in the case of a married ex-courtesan, namely, that of adultery.

Thus Lew's lies gave substance to my vague doubts, and I started to . . .' He broke off and looked around.

The door had burst open and Ma Joong came rushing inside.

'Bluewhite is in the Chancery, sir! She says she absolutely must speak to you.'

Judge Dee darted a quick glance at his excited lieutenant.

'I would certainly like to make her acquaintance,' he said calmly. 'However, there's no time now. We must proceed to the tribunal at once. We are late, and Chiao Tai is waiting for us there.'

'She said it's terribly important, sir!' Ma Joong protested.

'Tell her to wait, then. Come along!'

The judge descended the stairs, followed by his two lieutenants. While passing the chancery on the ground floor, Ma Joong slipped inside.

He rejoined Judge Dee and Tao Gan when they were about to ascend the sedan chair, in front of the gatehouse.

'I told her to wait, sir,' he reported with a crestfallen look. 'She seemed very angry. And she refused to tell me what it was all about.'

'She is a very independent young woman,' Judge Dee said and climbed into the sedan chair. When they were being carried away, he asked:

'What about those scavengers, Ma Joong?'

His tall lieutenant clasped his hand to his forehead.

'I clean forgot to tell you!' he exclaimed, annoyed at himself. 'All went well, sir. Our men arrested about sixty of them. It turned out that there were only two ringleaders, an ex-chief of a robber band and a renegade Taoist priest. They had been planning to organize a popular uprising, under the guise of a religious, anti-government movement. They wanted to take over the old city, plunder to their heart's delight, then clear out with the loot. The two ringleaders will be beheaded tonight. The others we let go, after a dressing-down they'll remember for a long time to come! To my great regret, sir, I have to report that Doctor Lew did not know about the plot. Guess why he frequented the scoundrels, sir! Just because he wanted them to inform him if they came upon a corpse that showed unusual symptoms of the sickness! I can't make out the bastard at all!'

'I had Lew arrested one hour ago,' the judge told him. Then he gave Ma Joong an account of what he had discovered in the Mei residence. When he had finished, he looked anxiously up at the sky. Shaking his head dubiously, he said:

'I still think the clouds are less stationary than before. And the air is even more humid than at noon. I still haven't given up hope that the rain will come, at last.'

They descended from the chair in front of the high gate of the military tribunal. Since martial law had been declared in the capital, all criminal cases had to be dealt with here instead of in the Municipal Tribunal or in Judge Dee's own High Court. The guards presented arms and a captain in full dress led the judge to the reception room. Chiao Tai came to meet him.

After he had invited the judge to be seated at the simple tea table, Chiao Tai presented to him the captain who would look after the court procedure. While the judge was sipping his tea, the captain explained all the details respectfully. By and large the procedure was the same as that followed in a civilian court, but greatly simplified. It was about eleven when Chiao Tai and Ma Joong led the judge and Tao Gan to the court.

The large hall was lit by torches, military fashion. Against the back wall stood rows of long halberds, peaks and spears, and in front of them was a raised platform with the bench: a high table covered by a piece of scarlet cloth. To the left and right stood a dozen military police with drawn swords. In the corner two orderlies were seated face to face at a small table littered with rolls of blank paper and writing instruments. They would act as scribes, noting down the proceedings verbatim.

Chiao Tai took the judge up to the platform, and pulled out the high armchair behind the bench. The judge seated himself, and Chiao Tai stood himself at Judge Dee's right side, Ma Joong on his left. Tao Gan sat down on the stool at the end of the bench.

Chiao Tai barked an order at the captain. He advanced in front of the bench, saluted and announced:

'Everything is ready, sir!'

Judge Dee took the gavel.

'As Emergency Governor of the Imperial capital, I herewith declare the session open.' He rapped the gavel. 'This court shall deal with the murder of Mr Mei Liang, a merchant of this city. I shall first hear the accused, Doctor Lew. Have him led before me, Captain!'

The captain gave an order to the military police. Two soldiers marched off through the arched door opening on the left.

Judge Dee inspected the forms that lay before him. They were blanks made especially for the emergency. Since each sheet bore already the impression of the large red Imperial seal countersigned by the Prime Minister, each leaf was carefully numbered. Ordinarily every capital sentence pronounced in the empire had to be submitted to the Grand Council, then to the Emperor himself for the final approval. Now, however, the emergency rules allowed summary justice.

The two soldiers led Doctor Lew before the bench. After he had knelt, the judge spoke:

'Doctor Lew, you have delivered false testimony twice. First when you stated that Mr Lei had died at or about ten o'clock in the evening, and the second time when you stated that Mrs Mei had not been a courtesan, but belonged to a distinguished family. Why did you make those statements, knowing full well that they were false? You stand accused of being concerned in the murder of Mr Mei, and I advise you to tell the truth and nothing but the truth.'

Doctor Lew raised his head. He was pale, but his voice was firm when he replied:

'This person denies emphatically having been concerned in the murder of Mr Mei, but he confesses that he did give your lordship wrong information. I was

145

foolish enough to believe the fancy tale Mrs Mei foisted on me. I was fully aware of the fact that she had been a courtesan, but I believed that she was an honest woman regardless, and genuinely in love with her husband, and——'

The judge rapped his gavel.

'I want an orderly statement. You have said that on the night in question you had dinner with Mr Mei, and that Mrs Mei attended upon you both. Begin from there!'

'After I had taken leave of Mr Mei, I went indeed to the housemaster's room, my lord. After I had given him the medicine, however, I decided there was nothing to worry about, and I went home.'

'So your story of hearing Mrs Mei scream in the east wing, and of your rushing to her and so on, all that was a lie?'

'Yes, my lord. I humbly apologize. I went back to the Mei mansion very early the next morning, on my way to another patient, just to see how the old housemaster was getting along. I knew that he was the only servant left in the house, and I was worried about him. Mrs Mei opened the door herself and told me that he was all right and would be up and about at noon. Yet she seemed very upset. She dragged me to a side room, and told me an astonishing tale.

'She said that, after she had seen her husband up to his library the evening before, she had decided to pass the night in the guest-room downstairs. For she was worried about his health and wanted to be near at hand, in case he should want something. Shortly after midnight, she woke up. Her husband had come into the room. He told her he had been unable to sleep, and was not feeling well. She wanted to get up to make a cup of tea for him, when he suddenly clutched at his throat and gasped for air. Before she could rush to his assistance he had toppled over, and his head struck a corner of the carved leg of the bedstead. She knelt by his side, and found he was dead.'

Lew paused. Looking up at the judge, he said earnestly:

THE JUDGE QUESTIONS A SUSPECT

'I believed her, my lord. I knew that Mr Mei did indeed have a weak heart, and he had been working much too hard, lately. Then, however, she went on that she was terribly worried that people would start gossiping if she told the true facts. Neither she nor her husband ever used the guest-room, she said, and malicious people would whisper that evidently her husband had surprised her there with a lover, and that the lover had struck him down. I thought that was rather far-fetched. I asked to see the body, but she said she had dragged it to the stairs in the hall. Would I help her, and tell the coroner that her husband had fallen down the staircase after dinner the night before and that she had then called me at once? I hesitated, but she . . . she is a very persuasive woman, my lord. She practically pushed me outside, saying, "Go now and fetch the coroner. If we wait too long, he'll get suspicious!" '

Doctor Lew wiped his moist face with his sleeve. Even in this high-ceilinged hall the heat was oppressive. He resumed:

'Now I come to the most painful part of my confession, my lord. I want to state formally that I fully realize that, by making this statement, I lay myself open to the charge of suppressing vital evidence. But the truth must be told. Well, I fetched the coronor, and told him that I had tried to find him the previous night; I could safely say that, for I knew he had to go every night to the communal pyre. Upon entering the hall, together with the coroner and his assistant, however, I got a terrible shock. I saw at once that Mei's skull had been crushed by a fearful frontal blow, a wound that could never have been caused by his hitting his head on the corner of the bedstead. Moreover, the suicide-scene had been so carefully set up, that I suspected that there had been an accomplice. Some blood and matter had even been smeared on the top of the newel! While the coroner was conducting his examination, I was thinking furiously. Now I understood that Mrs Mei's remarks about people gossiping about her husband having surprised her with a lover, were founded on truth: the truth, with a few judicious alterations! I realized the predicament I was in: she had made me an accomplice to murder! The only way out was to tell the coroner then and there that I was a fool, and denounce Mrs Mei. But . . .' He suddenly fell silent.

'Why didn't you do so, then?' Judge Dee asked evenly.

Doctor Lew hesitated. He cleared his throat a few times, before he began, haltingly:

'Well, my lord, before the coroner was through, she called me. We . . . we had a talk, in the side-room. She begged me on her knees to save her. Her husband had indeed caught her with her lover, they had quarreled, and the other man had hit Mei. He had intended to stun him, then to flee. They had been distracted with fear when they saw he was dead, and after a long consultation had hit upon the suicide-scheme. She told me that no one would ever suspect that Mei hadn't actually fallen down the steep staircase, and . . .'

'Who was her lover?' the judge cut him short.

'She wouldn't tell me, sir. I——' Suddenly he jumped up and clasped his hand to his forehead. 'Merciful Heaven!' he shouted. 'What an incredible fool I am! She will of course say it was me!' He fell to his knees again. 'Don't believe that woman, my lord! I beseech you, don't believe her! She is a depraved, deceitful creature, she——'

Judge Dee raised his hand.

'You are a very clever man, Lew!' he remarked coldly. 'I never doubted that. Captain, let the orderlies read out the accused's statement.'

The two men read out their notes in a sing-song voice, occasionally stopping to make a small correction where their records differed. The captain gave the document to Lew, who impressed his thumbmark on it. The doctor wanted to address the court again, but on a sign from Judge Dee the two soldiers grabbed his arms and dragged him outside.

'The dirty rat!' Chiao Tai whispered at Ma Joong. 'He hopes to put all the blame on his mistress, and get off with a stiff term in prison.'

149

The judge rapped his gavel.

'Lead the accused, Mrs Mei, before me, Captain,' he ordered.

The two soldiers came back at once, together with an elderly woman, dressed in black. It was the matron of the municipal women's jail.

'I beg to report, my lord,' she spoke, 'that the prisoner Mrs Mei is ill. She vomited several times, and I think she is running a fever. I advised her to request medical attention, and file a petition for a deferred hearing. But she wouldn't listen to me. She insisted on appearing in court as soon as she was summoned. What is your lordship's pleasure?'

The judge reflected a moment, vexedly tugging at his beard. Then he spoke:

'Since a brief statement will suffice now, you can bring her before me. But warn the coroner to examine her directly after the hearing.'

Judge Dee looked worriedly at Mrs Mei as she slowly advanced to the bench, very slender in her long white mourning robe. The matron had wanted to support her, but she had refused peremptorily. As she made to kneel, the judge said quickly:

'The accused is allowed to remain standing. This court now . . .'

'I killed my husband,' she interrupted him in a strange, hoarse voice. Fixing the judge with her large, too brilliant eyes she went on: 'I killed him, because I couldn't stand any longer the ineffectual attentions of that old man. I had married him because . . .' Her voice trailed off. She raised her head, the blue stones in her ear-pendants sparkling in the light of the torches. Looking over Judge Dee's head, into some unseen distance, she went on: 'I married him because life owed me a large debt. I was fifteen when I was sold to the brothel in the old city. I was beaten and kicked, humiliated and maltreated in every conceivable way. I was cruelly whipped, and compelled to beg for more. It was . . .' She put her hands to her face.

When she spoke again, her voice had regained some of its former rich timbre.

150

'Then I met someone who loved me. I was happy, for some time. Then I found our love was not enough to even the debt. I wanted more than love alone. So I married Mei. I then had everything I wanted . . . except love. I had lovers, many lovers. Mostly I found them clumsy louts who left me more miserable than before. The others . . . I felt soiled by their greedy lust, degraded by their shameless demands for money. My husband discovered my affairs, and his pity humiliated me. Humiliated me more than the worst whippings in the brothel. And after I had killed him, I had to beg for pity, beg that mean doctor, had to promise I would agree to his sordid proposals. . . . I always wanted more. And the more I got, the more I lost. I fully realize that now. Too late.'

A racking cough shook her frame.

'I am sick and tired of it all,' she stammered. 'Sick and tired . . . tired . . .'

She began to sway on her feet. After one forlorn look at the judge she collapsed on the stone floor.

The matron squatted down by her side and deftly loosened the front of her white robe. All of a sudden she jumped up, staggered back, and, covering her mouth with her sleeve, she pointed, horrified, at the tell-tale spots that covered Mrs Mei's neck and bosom. The captain drew back, away from the writhing woman. Her limbs shook convulsively. Then she lay still.

Judge Dee had risen from his chair. Leaning over the bench, he stared at the distorted face of the dead woman. He sat down and gave a sign to the captain. The captain shouted an order to the guards at the entrance. They hurriedly went outside.

The deadly silence that reigned in the hall was suddenly broken by a low, rumbling sound from afar off. No one seemed to notice it.

The guards came back with a reed mat. They covered their mouths and noses with their neckcloths, then they spread the mat over the dead body. The captain came up to the bench and told the judge: 'I ordered the guards to call the scavengers, sir.'

Judge Dee nodded. Then he said in a tired voice:
'Have the accused Hoo Pen led before me.'

XIX

The squat, broad shape of Hoo appeared in the
arched door opening, escorted by two soldiers. He
wore a hunter's hood on his head, and a long brown
riding robe, fastened with a leather belt. Evidently he
had been preparing to go out hunting when he was
arrested. Since no formal charge had been made against
him yet, he had been allowed to retain his own clothes
in jail.

He remained standing there a moment, somberly sur-
veying the hall. The soldier nudged him, and he walked
on in his shambling, awkward gait. He cast a casual
look at the reed mat, then walked on to the bench.

'Kneel here on this side!' the captain ordered him
quickly. He pointed with his sword to the corner of
the platform, as far as possible from the mat that covered the dead woman.

Judge Dee rapped his gavel.

'Hoo Pen,' he said gravely, 'you stand accused of
having murdered Mr Lei Liang, by striking him on the
head with a heavy ink-slab, in the guest-room of his
own house.'

Ma Joong and Chiao Tai exchanged a bewildered
look. Tao Gan sat up straight in his chair, fixing the
judge with an incredulous stare.

Hoo lifted his large head.

'So she betrayed me!' he said dully.

Judge Dee leaned forward in his chair.

'No,' he said quietly, 'she did not betray you. You

152

betrayed yourself. Last night, when I came to see you.'

Hoo fastened his eyes on the judge. He opened his mouth to speak, but Judge Dee went on quickly:

'When you were telling me and my assistant the true story of the Willow Pattern, you were evidently laboring under a strong emotion. You told it as if it happened to you yourself instead of to your great-grandfather, and a hundred years ago. Admittedly it is a pathetic tale. But you must have heard it told and retold uncounted times in the family circle. Why should this old tale of bygone days disturb you so? I suspected that you too had once redeemed a courtesan, probably sacrificing the last portion of your family fortune, and that she had left you to marry a rich man.'

He paused Hoo remained silent. He glared broodingly at the judge from under his thick eyebrows.

'Second,' Judge Dee resumed, 'when I informed you that Mr Yee was dead, you at once inquired about his eye. Now, the street jingle about the impending doom of the three houses, Mei, Hoo and Yee, mentions three ways of dying, in the ambiguous, oracular language those jingles always employ. Namely, by losing one's bed, by losing one's eye, and by losing one's head. The jingle did not specify to whom of the three each manner of dying applied. Yee had been killed by a fearful blow that destroyed the left half of his face. The killer had left in a hurry, without taking time, of course, to verify how the blow had affected Yee's eye. It struck me that you inquired at once after Yee's eye, remarking at the same time that you might die by losing your head. I thought that very strange, for your remark implied that you were very sure that Mr Mei had died by what the street song called "losing his bed". But Mei had died by falling down a staircase! I couldn't make head or tail of it. I didn't try to draw any conculsions, but I kept the facts in mind.'

The judge leaned back in his chair. Slowly caressing his sidewhiskers, he continued:

'Thereafter, however, I learned from a reliable source that Mrs Mei had been a courtesan, of a brothel in the old city. And that she had been bought by an unknown

153

person, whom she subsequently left for the wealthy Mr Mei. These events bore a striking similarity to the story of the Willow Pattern you told about your great-grand-father. It brought to mind a curious incident. When Mrs Mei came to see me, she winced when she noticed the Willow Pattern on a plate with cakes I offered her. And, more curious still, a puppeteer told me that a pros-titute called Sapphire had disappeared from a brothel in the old city, under mysterious circumstances. Sap-phire—the name of the courtesan your ancestor had bought out! And Mrs Mei showed a marked preference for that same stone. Odd coincidences. Yet I did not consider these facts as evidence that you were the man who had bought Mrs Mei out, and that you had re-mained her lover even after her marriage to Mei, with the implication that Mei instead of having died an acci-dental death had been murdered by the two of you. In the first place, I had no proof that Mei had indeed been murdered, and moreover I refused to believe that a worldly-wise and experiencd man like Mei would have married a depraved woman. I did have you arrested, but that was because of quite another charge that had been brought against you.'

Now Hoo wanted to speak, but the judge raised his hand.

'No, listen to me. I have a definite purpose in telling you all this. Well, tonight everything became clear. I discovered that Mr Mei had been brutally done to death. The murderer had bashed in the old man's head with a heavy ink-slab, and just before or after the deed he had kicked and beaten his victim in a ferocious manner. The body was covered by bad bruises, which we had wrongly ascribed to his hitting the edges of the steps while falling down. Then I also knew for sure why you had connected Mei's death with "losing his bed"; you interpreted that term as meaning that Mei died by losing his nuptial couch, because of his wife committing adultery. That meant that you had been Mrs Mei's lover, and that you murdered him when the old man surprised you with his wife in the guest-room. And thus the full meaning of your interpretation of the jingle was clarified. Mei had died by "losing his bed". If Yee's death had involved his losing his eye, the logical consequence was that *you* would lose your head; meaning that Mei's murder would be discovered and that you would die on the scaffold.

'Finally, the fact that it was you who had bought out Mrs Mei explained why Mei had kept the antecedents of his wife secret; it was not his secret alone, but also yours. A drama of conflicting passions among the leaders of the "old world", a world now rapidly fading away.'

The judge paused. Hoo's face was taut, but he did not speak.

'I explain all this to you, Mr Hoo, because I consider it my duty to Mrs Mei to prove that I discovered your guilt entirely by myself, and not through her betraying you. When she was standing here before my bench a few minutes ago, she didn't as much as mention your name. On the contrary, she insisted that it had been she who had murdered her husband. Because she had got tired of his attentions.'

Hoo came to his feet. Grasping the edge of the bench with his large hairy hands, he rasped:

'Where is she?'

'She is dead,' the judge said soberly. 'After she had made her confession she died right here. Of the plague.'

He pointed at the reed mat.

Hoo turned around and stared at the reed mat with wide eyes, his bushy eyebrows knit in a deep frown. His lips moved but no sound came forth. Again a faint rumble of thunder sounded afar off.

Suddenly Hoo uttered a half-suppressed, nearly animal moan. He stepped up to the reed mat. The captain rushed up to him to hold him back, but Judge Dee shook his head. Hoo lifted the edge of the mat, uncovering her arm, and took her slender white hand in his. Having stroked it gently, he then removed with infinite care the ring set with the sapphire, kissed it, and put it on his own little finger. After he had covered the hand again he rose, and resumed his former place

A MAN MEETS HIS DEAD MISTRESS

in front of the bench. Looking up at the judge, he said in a toneless voice:

'I beg to be allowed to wear this ring on the scaffold. I gave it to her when I had redeemed her.' When Judge Dee nodded his assent, Hoo bent his head and went on slowly, his eyes on the ring: 'She was still a young girl then. . . . A small, frightened girl. Her name was Sapphire, the same as that of the courtesan my great-grandfather had bought. "This is no coincidence," I told her, "it's the will of Heaven. Your love will make up for all the suffering the Sapphire of old caused my family."' He shook his large head. 'Why did she change, after our first happy years? Was it because she could not forget that I had bought her over the counter, so to speak? I don't know. When she left me, she did so with only a few words. "Mei is rich and you are poor," she said. "Life still owes me so much. . . . Brocade dresses, costly jewels, many maids to do my bidding. . . ." That is what she said.'

Turning the ring round on his finger, he went on:

'Yet, all the luxury Mei gave her did not make her happy. She had love affairs, many of them. I was sad, because I knew it meant she was unhappy, and lonely. One day, she called me. She said she had not been able to forget me, the man who had redeemed her. Did she mean it? I didn't know. I only knew that I was happy again. Then the sickness came. I told her she should leave, but she said no, for with the servants away, and old Mei gadding about in the market the whole day, we could meet more often. But last week she said: "This can't go on. I must leave this city, a city of death and decay. I want to start anew, in a far-away place." "Can I go with you?" I asked. "I don't know," she replied wearily. "I love you, but you would always remind me of the past. The past I want to forget."'

He fell silent. Judge Dee had been listening, sitting motionless in his armchair. Now he asked:

'What happened exactly on the fatal night?'

Hoo looked up, startled from his thoughts.

'What happened, you say? She had told me to come towards midnight. To the guest-room, as usual. Old

157

Mei had gone up to sleep long before, she said. We had left the bedcurtains drawn back, the only light came from the candle on her dressing-table. Suddenly the moon door opened, and old Mei came inside. He was dressed in his houserobe, his tousled grey head bare. "Kill him!" she told me. "I can't stand the sight of him. Not any longer!" I got up, but old Mei shook his head. "You needn't kill me, Hoo," he said. "Take her away with you. You bought her, she belongs rightfully to you." She jumped up and went to revile him, but he raised his hand. "I know that you have been unhappy here," he said, "and your going away with Hoo is your last chance. Perhaps you'll find what you are looking for, at last." Shaking his head, he added with that sanctimonious air of his: "If you knew how I pity you!" Those words cut me to the quick. He forgive her? Only I had the right to forgive her! In a blind rage I grabbed the ink-slab, struck him down and kicked that miserable thin body of his about. I stopped only when she put her arms round me, and told me to desist.'

He passed his hand over his moist face.

'We sat down together on the edge of the bed, without saying a word. What was there to say? At last she spoke up. "I have decided that you shall go with me," she said. "We shall drag the body to the hall, to the foot of the marble staircase. Make it appear that he fell down, earlier in the night. After a few days we shall leave. Together." We dragged the body to the hall and arranged a few clues there to prove that he had indeed had an accident. Then I left, through the garden door. That's all.'

Four black men, their heads covered by hoods, entered the court hall. They rolled the body in the reed mat, with the ease of much practice. Then they wrapped it up in a sheet of canvas. Hoo's eyes followed them as they carried their burden away.

Judge Dee gave a sign to the orderlies. Again the two men read aloud their notes in their high-pitched sing-song voices. They were nearly through when a flash of lightning lit up the high windows. There was a deafening thunder-clap, followed by the clatter of rain against the oil-paper of the windowpanes.

The judge turned round in his chair.

'The rain has come,' he said to his lieutenants. 'At last!'

The captain had taken the document drawn up by the orderlies. Now he held it up for Hoo, who put his thumbmark on it. Judge Dee rose. He straightened his robe and spoke:

'Hoo Pen, there has also been brought forward against you another capital charge. I need not go into that, however, for your confessing to the murder of Mr Mei Liang, a good man and benefactor of the people, amply suffices for your indictment. This court herewith sentences the accused Hoo Pen to death by decapitation. Martial law requires that this sentence is executed forthwith.'

He sat down again, took up his writing-brush and filled in the official form. Having impressed his seal on it, he turned around in his chair and handed it to Chiao Tai: 'You, Colonel, will immediately take the necessary measures, together with Colonel Ma. Tao Gan shall witness the execution on my behalf, and draw up the official report.' He rapped his gavel.

Two soldiers stepped up to Hoo, but he did not see them. His eyes were on the ring on his finger. Slowly he turned it round and round. The large sapphire sparkled with a blue light. One of the soldiers tapped him on his shoulder. He turned around and meekly let them lead him away, his broad shoulders sagging in the wide hunter's cloak.

Judge Dee spoke:

'This court shall convene again early tomorrow morning. Then the accused Doctor Lew shall be sentenced to a long term in prison, for having delivered false testimony, for having suppressed important evidence, and for unprofessional behavior. The court is adjourned.'

Again he rapped his gavel. He rose and walked to the door, his arms folded in his wide sleeves. All present stood stiffly at attention.

XX

The sentries at the gate of the Military Tribunal had fixed an improvised canvas roofing over the seat of Judge Dee's sedan chair. While the soldiers were carrying him away he leaned back in the pillows, letting his right hand hang outside so that he could feel the cool raindrops.

Suddenly he realized that he was completely worn out. He tried to concentrate on the session of the tribunal, but the hall with the flickering torches seemed as unreal and evasive as a scene from a dream, only half remembered. His thoughts became confused, they turned round and round. While everything grew blurred he had the horrible sensation that he had been carried along in this sedan chair for days on end, and that it would go on and on, in a circle from which there was no escape. A hollow, sick feeling rose from the pit of his stomach. Lifting his hands, he pressed his fingertips hard against his temples. Slowly the dizziness went away. But there remained a feeling of utter fatigue, utter futility. He asked himself whether this was only the normal reaction to the three weeks of mental and physical strain. Or was it a sign that old age was catching up with him?

Sunk in somber thought, he idly looked at the empty, wet streets. Here and there lights were going on behind the windows of the dark, silent houses. Soon the Court would come back, and the capital would resume its normal routine, become again the bustling metropolis, bristling with activity. The thought could not dispel his deep gloom.

A loud, drawn-out cry made him suddenly sit up. There followed the rattle of a wooden clapper, just ahead. The wet, wrinkled face of a very old man appeared in the cone of light from the chair's swinging lantern. The old man held up a basket heaped with folded sheets of oiled paper. His bare arms, sticking out of the tattered sleeves, were pitifully thin.

'Out of the way!' the soldiers barked.

'Halt!' the judge called to them. 'I'll take one,' he told the vendor. It was the first street hawker he had seen in three weeks.

'Five coppers! Four apiece if you take two, noble lord!' There was a sly glint in the old man's eyes as he looked up at the judge from under his tufted grey eyebrows. 'The very best oil-paper, protects you against the rain, and against the sun too! Take two, my lord, tonight the price'll go up!'

The judge accepted one sheet and took a silver piece from his sleeve. 'Good luck!' he told him.

The old hawker snatched the silver and scurried away over the wet cobblestones, afraid that this crazy lord would repent of his generosity. At a safe distance he began to sound his clapper vigorously again.

With a smile the judge spread the oiled paper out over his wet boots. A warm glow of pride had swept away all his weariness and anxiety—an immense pride in the people he was privileged to serve. For three long weeks they had been cowering in their miserable hovels and shanties, half-starved, paralyzed by a dumb fear, at the mercy of the implacable enemy that was stalking about among them, unseen. Yet now, at the very first sign of a change for the better, they came out again at once, unbeaten, eager to haggle over the few coppers needed for their meager bowl of rice.

Arrived back at the palace, he answered good-humoredly the happy greetings of the orderlies and clerks he met while ascending the stairs to the fourth floor.

He went out on the marble terrace at once. Standing at the balustrade, he saw through the steady drizzle more and more lights going on all over the city. Then there came the deep bronze voice of the large gong of the Buddhist temple. A service of thanksgiving had begun.

The judge went inside, took off his heavy ceremonial dress and replaced his winged headwear by a small skullcap. Clad only in his thin under-robe, he sat down behind his desk. He rubbed ink, took up his brush and jotted down a message addressed to his First Lady, in the formal style prescribed for correspondence between husband and wife.

Pressure of official business prevented me from communicating with you earlier. Today the rain has come, and that means the end of the Black Death, and of the emergency. I trust I shall be able to let all of you return to the city in the near future. There were some unexpected developments but, mainly through the untiring efforts of my three lieutenants, the situation remained well in hand. Greetings also to my Second and Third, and to the children.

He scrawled his signature, then leaned back in his chair. Thinking fondly of his wives and children, he felt he ought to add a postscript, a few lines of a more personal character. Listening to the patter of the rain, he groped for a suitable phrasing. Before he knew it he had dozed off.

He was awakened by the entrance of his three lieutenants, tired and wet. Tao Gan handed the judge a rolled-up document. Motioning them to be seated, Judge Dee glanced through the official report, written out in Tao Gan's small, neat hand. Hoo had been executed in the square of the communal pyre. When the executioner was baring his neck, Hoo had cast a long look at the pyre, spluttering in the drizzle. 'We are leaving together,' he had said. Those had been his last words.

Tao Gan took the sapphire ring from his sleeve. 'This trinket was taken off Hoo's body. It should be added to the assets of the Mei estate, I presume?'

'Yes. Make a large pot of strong tea, Tao Gan.'

While Tao Gan busied himself about the tea table in the corner, Chiao Tai pushed his helmet back and said:

'When I was taking Hoo up to the scaffold, sir, I asked him why exactly he had killed Yee. He gave me that blank stare of his, and said: "Yee was a cruel devil. He got what he deserved." Shouldn't this admission of his guilt be entered into the record, sir? Just for the sake of completeness?'

The judge shook his head.

'No, it wasn't meant as an admission of guilt,' he said evenly. 'For Hoo did not kill him.' Seeing the astonished faces of his lieutenants, he went on: 'Hoo could not have known that Coral was with Yee that particular night. Didn't she state that the bamboo curtains were down? Even if we assume that Hoo had been watching the gallery from across the canal, he could not have seen that anything special was going on there. And we can't assume that he swam across and climbed onto the balcony just to spy on Yee, and happened to arrive there at exactly the moment that Yee was going to kill Coral. No, my friends, that would have been too much of a coincidence! Also, Hoo was a very strong man, but of squat build, while Yee was taller than average. And the wound had been inflicted from above, by a person as tall or taller than Yee.'

'But Coral said she had seen Hoo standing behind the bamboo curtain, sir!' Tao Gan exclaimed.

'That is what she thought,' said Judge Dee. 'She had been thinking of Hoo, because Yee made her stand naked on the couch. But this time the devil did that only to gloat over her embarrassment, not to tease Hoo. For there was only one candle, and the bamboo curtains were down. In her excitement Coral did not take in those facts. She saw vaguely a large shadow, and naturally assumed it was Hoo.'

'Who killed Yee then?' Ma Joong burst out.

The judge gave him a keen look.

'After I had heard Coral's story,' he said, 'I worked out a theory. It would fit all the facts, but I had no means of verifying it. I hoped, or trusted rather, that

163

tonight some development would occur that would prove my theory. Well, it did occur, exactly as I had expected. That caused me great pleasure. And not only because it confirmed my theory, mind you.' He took the cup Tao Gan offered him, but it was too hot and he set it down and looked out.

'It's getting to be a real downpour!' he exclaimed. He clapped his hands. When the orderly appeared, he told him: 'Send a man to the guards at the west city gate at once, and tell them to close the sluices.' Then he resumed:

'Let's have a second look at Coral's statement. She said that Yee had met her and her sister in the market, and that he took Coral aside. Now Bluewhite is a clever girl, she must have guessed that something was wrong. The story Coral tried to foist on her will not have been too clever, I imagine, for she is a simple, artless child. Anyway, Bluewhite became suspicious, and decided to keep an eye on her sister. When Coral left that night, Bluewhite secretly followed her. Right to Yee's mansion.

'She saw Yee admit her sister by the small door in the iron gate. She was at a loss what to do, for there is no other means of entering that huge old fortress. However, she is a resourceful girl. She went down to the bank near the bridge, and stripped in the shrubbery. She was going to swim along the bank to the balcony of the gallery, and try to gain access to the house from that side. Since she didn't want to go unarmed, she took one of the iron balls, and tied it into her hair knot. Then she wound her scarf tightly around her head. That would keep the ball in place, and her hair dry.'

He took a sip from his tea. Casting a quick glance at Ma Joong, he continued:

'For a trained acrobat like her, it was an easy job to climb up along one of the pillars, and tall and lithe as she is, getting up on the ledge wasn't too difficult either. Standing there she heard Yee rave about his having whipped their mother to death, and about killing Coral in the same manner. When she saw, through the bamboo curtain, that Yee lashed Coral across her breast, she untied the scarf, put the ball inside, raised the curtain and stepped over the windowsill.

'Yee had turned around, because he had heard something. Then he got a terrible shock. The stark naked, dripping wet woman with her long, dishevelled hair must have appeared to him an avenging ghost from the Nether World. Then he realized that it was even worse than a ghost: it was Coral's sister, not a meek, defenseless girl, but a trained fighter, with a deadly weapon in her hand. Just like most excessively cruel people, Yee was a coward. He let the whip drop and screamed for help. You'll remember, Tao Gan, that his mouth was wide open. Then she felled him with one terrible stroke of the weighted scarf. The force of the blow smacked him backwards into his armchair.'

He paused, and watched for a moment the pouring rain.

'I feel certain,' he resumed, 'that so much actually happened. What follows now is largely guesswork. I suppose that, having killed Yee, her rage suddenly abated. She looked in horror at what she had done. One couldn't expect her to know that killing Yee had been a clear case of manslaughter, completely justifiable for he had been on the point of murdering her sister, in the same hideous manner as he had murdered their mother. When she saw the blood on her scarf, she got into a real panic. She threw the iron ball into the canal, and the stained scarf on the floor. Then she stepped on the ledge outside, let herself down the pillar, and swam back. She dressed on the bank, and went to the tavern. That's where you met her, Ma Joong.'

'Now I understand why she ignored her father then!' Ma Joong exclaimed. 'She was sore at him because he had never told her the truth about her mother's death, while he had taken her sister into his confidence!'

The judge nodded.

'She resolved never to tell him what she had done. Later she remembered having left the scarf on the scene of the killing. She began to worry whether she or her sister had perhaps left other clues too. We know

165

that, except for Coral's ear-pendant and the red stone, there were none. For the maid Cassia had found the wet spots on the windowsill, and she had wiped them off carefully, because she thought these traces pointed to Hoo. But Bluewhite did not know that, of course. So she decided she would go back there and enter the gallery in the same manner as before. She had not reckoned with the fact, however, that now the canal wasn't any more a mass of quiet, practically stagnant water. The sluices had been opened, and there was a strong current.'

He cast a quick glance at Ma Joong.

'You were born and bred in the water district, my friend. You ought to know that, when there is a bend in a water course, the current is always strongest along the outer side of the curve. I often noticed that fact when, standing on a bridge, I followed the course of pieces of driftwood. Moreover, on the inner side of the bend, downstream from the Halfmoon Bridge, there rises the steep wall of the Yee mansion. That narrows down the current, and increases its pull towards the outer side of the bend. The girl never reached her destination. The current carried her across the canal over to the opposite side, and in the bight under Hoo's balcony she got entangled in the weeds. After you had saved her, Ma Joong, she had to make up a story, and quick too. Do you remember whether you mentioned Hoo at all?'

Ma Joong scratched his chin.

'Come to think of it, I did,' he said ruefully. 'Made a feeble joke about Hoo having chucked her over the balcony.'

'Exactly. That gave her her cue. Well, after I had heard Coral's story, and formulated my theory, I made it a point to stress to Yuan that I would make Hoo's attempted rape of Bluewhite count heavily against him. I trusted that, if my theory was right, she would come to me and make a clean breast of it. For she is a decent girl, I understand, and she would never let a man be wrongly accused because of a faked story fabricated by her. There had been, of course, other facts that sup-

A YOUNG GIRL TAKES VENGEANCE

ported my theory. To begin with, when I left Hoo, he certainly wasn't in the mood for trying to rape a girl. He was waiting, not for Bluewhite, but for a message from Mrs Mei. Further, the scarf we found was only wet from water in the four corners, suggesting a swimmer having knotted it round the head—which pointed to a woman. Also, when Bluewhite fought off the scoundrels in the tavern, she had only one weighted sleeve.'

'And her hair was still wet,' Ma Joong muttered. With a sigh of admiration, he added: 'And that's why she drank like a fish! What a wench!'

'You'd better go to the Chancery, Ma Joong,' the judge said dryly, 'and see whether she's still waiting there. If so, you might ask her yourself about the details of her adventure.'

Ma Joong jumped up and rushed outside without another word.

'She is a very impetuous and independent young woman,' Judge Dee told the others with a smile. 'What she needs is a good husband. That will make her settle down, I'd say.'

'Brother Ma will see to that all right!' Chiao Tai remarked with a broad grin. 'He should follow the ancient custom and marry her twin sister at the same time, as his Number Two. That'd give him a chance to prove his mettle!' He paused, rubbing his knees with a satisfied air. Suddenly he asked: 'Oughtn't we to make the wench tell the whole story in the tribunal, sir, and have her officially acquitted? Yee's death can't be filed as an unsolved murder case!'

The judge raised his thick eyebrows.

'Why shouldn't it? I don't want the private affairs of the future family of our friend Ma Joong to be bandied about in all the teahouses downtown. I shall have Yee's demise registered as murder committed by a person or persons unknown. I don't mind a bit having a few unsolved cases on my record.'

'So Brother Ma got hooked, at last!' Tao Gan said with his thin smile. 'And how!' Then, however, his face fell. Tugging at the hairs that grew from his left cheek, he resumed with a dejected face: 'So the Willow Pattern wasn't a clue, after all. Yee pushed the flower vase aside when he was eating the ginger, and later it dropped onto the floor accidentally.'

The judge gave his lieutenant a pensive look. Letting his long sidewhiskers glide through his fingers, he said slowly:

'No, I am not too sure about that, Tao Gan. The odds are that your reasoning about the significance of the broken vase as a clue still holds good. We shall never be able to prove it, though. Remember that Yee had screamed when he saw Bluewhite coming for him. And also that he did not know that Coral had fled. He will have assumed that the twin sisters would be discovered in the gallery by the maid or the young doorman. Since he was a vicious, spiteful man I think it quite possible that, having recognized the avenging fury, his last thought was to leave a clue to her identity. Therefore he deliberately smashed the flower vase. Not because it was decorated with the Willow Pattern, but for a much more obvious reason. Namely that it was blue-and-white porcelain. Pour me another cup, will you?'

POSTSCRIPT

Judge Dee was a historical person who lived from 630 to 700 A.D. In the earlier half of his long official career he distinguished himself as an eminent detector of crimes, and after his appointment to high office in the Imperial capital he became, through his sagacity and courage, one of the outstanding statesmen of the Tang period. The adventures narrated in the present novel—entirely fictitious—are supposed to have happened in the second phase of Judge Dee's career, when he had served about one year as President of the Metropolitan Court.

The introduction of the Willow Pattern in this Judge Dee novel is a conscious anachronism; as is well known, this decorative motif of blue-and-white pottery and porcelain originated in England in the 18th century. I could as well have employed a purely Chinese motif current in Judge Dee's own time, but preferred the Willow Pattern because, although it is one of the most popular ceramic designs ever used in England, in this particular form it is little known in China. Thus I hoped to give western readers the satisfaction of recognizing a theme so frequently found on English crockery, and to arouse the Chinese reader's interest in a western development of a Chinese decorative motif.

The precise origin of the Willow Pattern is an unsolved mystery. It has not yet been ascertained what Chinese model, if any, the famous English artist Thomas Turner followed in designing this motif for the Caughley Factory in Staffordshire, when he was working there from 1772 to 1799. Landscapes of country villas on the waterside planted with willow trees are frequently found on Chinese porcelain (see, for instance, plates 252 and 253 in W. G. Gulland *Chinese Porcelain,* vol. I, London, 1902), but as far as I know the particular design where the villa is connected by a bridge with a water-pavilion, and a person with a raised stick is pursuing two others crossing that bridge, has not yet been found on purely Chinese porcelain. Since, however, a bridge being crossed by two friends followed by a page carrying a seven-stringed lute (the favorite musical instrument of the literati; cf. Dr R. H. van Gulik *The Lore of the Chinese Lute,* Monumenta Nipponica Monographs, Sophia University, Tokyo, 1940) is a common Chinese motif, I suspect that an English designer mistook the lute for a stick or a sword, which gave rise to the 'legend' concerning the pattern. Bernard Watney aptly summarizes the situation in his *English Blue and White Porcelain of the Eighteenth Century* (London, 1963, p. 113): 'The Willow Pattern was not really an original Caughley chinoiserie, but merely the crystallization of a number of similar transfers used at the English porcelain factories from about 1760. This romantic vision of Cathay gained full popularity in its final form as a result of the mass production of cheap earthenware by Staffordshire potteries in the nineteenth century. The creation of a suitable legend heightened the appeal and ensured its continuity.' I may add that the 'legend' about the mandarin's daughter who fell in love with her father's poor secretary (related by Tao Gan on page 39 of the present novel) bears the hallmark of the pseudo-oriental romanticism popular in England and Western Europe during the second half of the eighteenth century; a lengthy version, complete with amatory verse, may be found in C. A. S. Williams *Outlines of Chinese Symbolism and Art Motives,* Shanghai, 1932, s.v. *willow.* After the English-made Willow Pattern ware had been sent to China, Chinese potters imitated it for re-export to the west, laboriously copying with their brushes the English transfer-printed design. 'The best-known Chinese porcelain with Willow decoration is the blue-and-white

Canton or "Nankin" ware, a utility ware of the early 19th century (or earlier) made for export. It is often thickly potted, sometimes even clumsy, and has been made continuously ever since its introduction. It was and still is made in three qualities; the highest quality having sharply distinct brush-work in dark blue, while the lowest quality has the familiar misty blue outline. This ware was very exactly copied in England by Josiah Spode II for export to Persia (1810-1815). Nankin Willow ware is quaint and often very charming, and is still sought by discriminating people.' (Quoted from F. St George Spendlove's article 'The Willow Pattern: English and Chinese' in *Far Eastern Ceramic Bulletin,* vol. VIII, no. 1, Boston, 1956.)

With regard to the adventures of 'Sapphire' related in this novel, I may remark that the reader will find full details about the role of the courtesan in Tang society in my book *Sexual Life in Ancient China, a preliminary survey of Chinese sex and society from ca. 1500 B.C. till 1644 A.D.* (E. J. Brill, Leiden, 1961), p. 171 *et seq.*

The art of fighting with loaded sleeves has survived till recent years. I was told during my stay in Peking in 1935 that the formidable reputation this art enjoys among the Chinese lower classes saved the lives of six western Catholic nuns during the Boxer troubles of 1900. The sisters were set upon by an angry mob when they were on their way to the fortified cathedral. Expecting to be slaughtered, they resignedly raised their folded hands, commending their souls to God. Suddenly one of the ruffians who was about to attack them shouted, 'Look out! They've loaded sleeves!' The mob drew back and made way for the sisters, who safely reached the cathedral. What happened was that, when the sisters raised their hands, the breviaries they were carrying in their sleeves swung to and fro; their attackers, who, through the vicious anti-foreign propaganda of the Boxers, believed all westerners capable of all conceivable mischief, concluded that the sisters had 'loaded sleeves'.

I may repeat here that in Judge Dee's time the Chinese did not wear pigtails; that custom was imposed on them after 1644 A.D. when the Manchus had conquered China. Before 1644 they let their hair grow long, and did it up in a top-knot. They wore caps both inside and outside the house. Tobacco and opium were introduced into China only many centuries later.

ROBERT VAN GULIK